"I ruined your wedding night."

When she didn't take the champagne flute, he pressed it into her hand, wrapping his fingers around hers. She could barely breathe as she looked up at him, feeling his large hand wrapped around her smaller one. He said in a low voice, "I am going to make it up to you tonight."

"H-How?" she stammered.

He stepped back, his gaze still intensely upon her. She felt butterflies in her stomach and nervously drank the rest of the delicious raspberry-infused champagne. But the butterflies only increased. With a sensual promise in his dark gaze, Xerxes silently refilled her champagne.

All about the author...
Jennie Lucas

JENNIE LUCAS had a tragic beginning for any would-be writer: a very happy childhood. Her parents owned a bookstore, and she grew up surrounded by books, dreaming about faraway lands. When she was ten, her father secretly paid her a dollar for every classic novel (*Jane Eyre, War and Peace*) that she read.

At fifteen, she went to a Connecticut boarding school on scholarship. She took her first solo trip to Europe at sixteen, then put off college and traveled around the U.S., supporting herself with jobs as diverse as gas-station cashier and newspaper advertising assistant.

At twenty-two, she met the man who would be her husband. For the first time in her life, she wanted to stay in one place, as long as she could be with him. After their marriage, she graduated from Kent State University with a degree in English, and started writing books a year later.

Jennie was a finalist in the Romance Writers of America's Golden Heart contest in 2003 and won the award in 2005. A fellow 2003 finalist, Australian author Trish Morey, read Jennie's writing and told her that she should write for Harlequin® Presents. It seemed like too big a dream, but Jennie took a deep breath and went for it. A year later, Jennie got the magical call from London that turned her into a published author.

Since then, life has been hectic—juggling a writing career, a sexy husband and two young children—but Jennie loves her crazy, chaotic life. Now, if she could only figure out how to pack up her family and live in all the places she's writing about!

For more about Jennie and her books, please visit her website at www.jennielucas.com.

Jennie Lucas

THE BRIDE THIEF

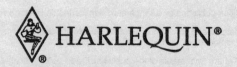

TORONTO • NEW YORK • LONDON
AMSTERDAM • PARIS • SYDNEY • HAMBURG
STOCKHOLM • ATHENS • TOKYO • MILAN • MADRID
PRAGUE • WARSAW • BUDAPEST • AUCKLAND

Recycling programs
for this product may
not exist in your area.

ISBN-13: 978-0-373-12965-2

THE BRIDE THIEF

First North American Publication 2011

Copyright © 2010 by Jennie Lucas

THE BRIDE THIEF

To my wonderful agent, Jennifer Schober,
with gratitude.

CHAPTER ONE

IT WAS a fairy tale come true.

Three months ago, Rose Linden had been struggling to pay her bills. Today, she no longer worked two jobs in San Francisco, scraping frozen rain off the window of the broken-down car she jump-started each night. As of an hour ago, she'd become a baroness, with the world at her manicured fingertips.

And Lars Växborg was her husband.

Rose glanced at her new husband across the enormous gilded ballroom of his castle in northern Sweden. The slender, blond baron looked sleek in his tuxedo, sipping champagne as he was deep in discussion with several young women.

She was his wife now. She should have been ecstatic. And yet, staring at Lars across the room, she suddenly found she couldn't breathe.

"Very fancy wedding, *Baroness*," her father teased, then frowned. "But why are you so skinny these days, peanut? You been sick or something?"

Her mother elbowed him in the ribs. "It's her wedding day," she hissed. "Rose looks beautiful!"

He looked her up and down accusingly. "She's skin and bone!"

Her mother patted her own full cheeks. "I dieted before my wedding to you, Albert. But of course—" she sighed "—that was five children ago. For heaven's sake, let Rose enjoy being thin, because it won't last!"

But Rose didn't laugh, as she normally would have while being teased by her large, loving family. Nor did she tell them that she hadn't lost weight on purpose. She just never felt like she could relax around Lars, even though—or perhaps *because*—he constantly assured her she was perfect in every way.

She'd told herself it was wedding day jitters, but though she'd already spoken her vows she was still feeling queasier by the minute. Was it because she hadn't eaten since yesterday? Or because the corset boning of the bodice of her wedding gown was laced too tightly, causing her breasts to spill over the top?

She should have felt like the perfect Cinderella bride, in full white skirts and with a diamond tiara sparkling above her long lace veil. But she still felt small and out-of-place in the castle. And her mother was a bloodhound where her children's emotions were concerned. She could already see Vera starting to frown. In a minute, she'd ask questions, questions Rose couldn't answer— not even to herself.

Trembling, Rose set down her crystal flute on the tray of a passing waiter. "I'm going out for some fresh air."

"We'll come with you."

"No. Please, I just need a minute. Alone—"

Turning, she fled the ballroom. She ran through the empty hallways of the castle and out into the dark winter's night. Once she was outside, she fell back heavily against the medieval door. It scraped against the stone before finally slamming shut with a sonorous bang that echoed into the white, ghostlike garden.

Rose closed her eyes, taking a deep breath that burned her lungs in the frozen February air.

She was married now.

She'd thought she would feel…different.

At twenty-nine, she'd long been an object of pity to her friends and siblings, all of whom were married except her youngest brother. Every time they'd said, "You're too picky" or "Who are you waiting for, Rose— Prince Charming?" Rose had cried in private, in her lonely single apartment, but she'd still kept faith. She was determined not to settle. She would wait for true love, even if it took forever.

Then Lars had walked into the San Francisco diner where she worked the morning shift. He'd sat down at the counter and ordered coffee and the breakfast plate special.

San Francisco was a cosmopolitan, colorful city, far more populated than the tiny coastal village to the south where Rose had grown up; but even for San Francisco, a man like Lars was unusual. He was a wealthy, handsome aristocrat who'd gone to Oxford, who had his own ancestral castle in Sweden. From the moment they'd met, he'd pursued Rose with reckless abandon.

Men had pursued her before, and she'd never been interested. But Lars's incredibly romantic, complimentary charm had swept her off her feet. A week ago, he'd proposed marriage. *"Let's elope today,"* he'd begged. *"I can't wait to have you as my wife."* After she'd accepted, he'd only grudgingly agreed to wait a week, long enough for her family to be able to attend. When she'd asked for a small wedding in her hometown, he'd arranged instead for her entire family—her grandmother, parents and her five siblings and their families—to fly to northern Sweden.

They'd had a magical wedding. And tonight, they'd make love for the first time.

Was that why Rose felt this sinking feeling inside, like the cratering of her soul? She was nervous. That had to be the reason she felt so ill. She had nothing to be scared about, she told herself fiercely. *Nothing*.

Still, the enormity of what she'd promised—pledging her life to Lars forever—made her skin feel cold in a way that had nothing to do with the ice and frost. She'd just married the man of her dreams, so why was her body still shaking as if preparing to flee? What was wrong with her?

Pushing away from the medieval door of the castle, she crossed the bridge over the frozen moat and walked into the silent, decorative garden with its ghostly cover of snow. Her white tulle skirts trailed lightly behind her, scattering powdery flakes that sparkled like diamonds in the moonlight.

The night was dark and clear. Looking up, she nearly gasped when she saw violent streaks of pale green light suddenly whip across the sky. *Northern lights*. She'd never seen anything so beautiful or so strange. Their magic caught at her soul. She closed her eyes.

"Please," she prayed softly, "let me have a happy marriage."

But when she opened her eyes, the northern lights were gone, leaving only a dark, empty sky behind.

"So," a deep voice said behind her, "you are the bride."

Rose whirled to face him, her skirts sweeping the snow.

A man, dark as shadow, stood in front of three black SUVs on the edge of the graveled courtyard. His black hair and long, black coat were illuminated in the moonlight, where he stood beside a pale, solitary rowan tree that was thick with frost and half-strangled in mistletoe.

Rose trembled as if she'd seen a ghost. She whispered, "Who are you?"

Without a word, he started walking toward her.

Something about his malevolent stare and the shadows of his face frightened her. Rose suddenly realized how far she'd wandered from the castle, and how alone she was. In the warm, glowing castle, she knew the ballroom was full of noise, with a chamber string orchestra and hundreds of laughing, tipsy guests. Would anyone even hear her if she screamed?

Oh, she was being silly. She was in *Sweden*, for heaven's sake! There was no safer, friendlier place than this!

Ignoring the instincts that told her to turn and run, Rose folded her arms over her white, corseted bodice. Lifting her chin, she waited for his answer.

The stranger stopped directly in front of her, his body inches away from hers. He was so muscular and broad-shouldered he had to be almost twice her weight. He was so tall that the top of her head barely reached his shoulder.

His black eyes gleamed down at her. "Are you alone out here, little one?"

A chill crept across the skin of her arms, bare beneath the white lace sleeves. She shook her head. "There are hundreds of people inside the ballroom."

His cruel, sensual lips curved upward.

"Ah, but you're not in the ballroom. You're alone. And do you not know," he said softly, "how cold a winter night can be?"

Cold. A shiver went through her. No matter how high the thermostat was set in the aging castle or how many sweaters she'd worn, no matter how many times Lars had assured her that she was perfect—that she could be nothing *but* perfect—she'd never once felt warm in the sparkling, exquisite beauty of his northern palace surrounded by ice. But she wasn't going to say that to a stranger. "I'm not afraid of a little snow."

"Such bravery." The stranger's black eyes traced over her body, burning her wherever they touched. "And yet you know why I've come."

"Yes, of course," she said, bewildered.

"But you do not run away?"

She blinked, even as her feet inched backward of their own volition, and said, "Why would I run?"

His black eyes searched hers as if sifting through her soul. "You actually take responsibility for your crime?"

His face was too brutal, his body too muscular to be handsome. But it was hard to get a good look at his face. In the shadows of the moonlit night, he was like a vampire sucking up every bit of light despite the illumination from the snow. And his darkness was more than the black of his hair, his eyes and his long coat. There was something in his posture that frightened her. A danger. *A threat.*

And yet she forced herself to hold still. She glanced back at the castle to reassure herself. Her husband and family were near. She had no reason to be afraid. She was so overwrought she was imagining things!

"By 'crime' do you mean the wedding?" she replied lightly. "It was perhaps a bit overdone but that's hardly a crime."

But the man didn't even smile. She cleared her throat.

"I'm sorry," she said. "I shouldn't joke. You must have traveled a long distance for our wedding, only to arrive an hour too late. That would make anyone upset."

"Upset?" he ground out.

"I'll get you some champagne inside," she urged. Her feet started inching back again toward the castle. "Lars will be so happy to see you."

The man barked a sudden laugh. "Is that another joke?"

Rose stopped. "Aren't you one of his friends?"

The man drew closer to her.

"No," he said. "I am not a friend."

His body towered over hers without touching her, leaving her in shadow. She felt his physical strength like a threat.

And suddenly, she knew that her instincts had been right all along.

She had to flee for safety—*now.*

"Excuse me," she choked out, stumbling back. "My husband's waiting for me. Hundreds of people—*security guards, policemen*—are waiting for our first dance as a married couple...."

The man's hand flew out to grab her upper arm over her translucent lace sleeve, gripping her tight, preventing her escape.

"Married?" he repeated in cold fury.

Why was he looking as if he might kill her for saying something so innocent and so obvious? "Yes, it's our— You're hurting me!"

His hand had tightened, gripping painfully into her arm. His black eyes stared down at her with deep, fathomless rage as he slowly looked from her breasts, which were pushed up by the tight bodice, to the enormous diamond ring sparkling on her left hand.

Finally, his eyes met hers, and it was like a blast of fire as he said in a low voice, "You both deserve to burn in hell for what you've done."

She gaped at him. "What? What are you talking about?"

With a brutal jerk, he pulled her so close to him that her wide tulle skirts whirled around his muscular legs.

"You know," he said in a low, grim voice. "And you know why I've come."

"I don't!" she panted, struggling in his brutal grip. "Are you insane? Let me go!"

An icy breeze lifted her veil above her blond chignon, up into the air, swirling around them both in the dark frozen night. She felt the latent power and hostility emanating off the stranger's strong body, and for a moment, she felt lost in a medieval nightmare of ice, fire and Vikings.

But this wasn't a dream! He held her tight, crushing her fruitless struggles.

"You are a liar, just as I knew you'd be," he hissed in her ear. She saw the ice crystals of their joined breath swirl like mist and smoke around them, before he pulled back to look down at her with hard eyes. "What I did not realize was that you would also be so beautiful."

"You've…you've made some kind of mistake." She licked her dry lips. His dark eyes fell to her mouth, tracing the movement of her tongue.

Her lips burned beneath his gaze, causing a scorching trail of fire to spread down her body, sizzling from her lips to her earlobes. To her breasts. To her core, coiling low in her belly.

"No mistake," he said roughly, his grip tightening on her shoulders. "You've committed a crime. Now you will pay."

"You're drunk—or crazy!"

Kicking his shins, she wrenched away from his grasp. Desperately, she fled toward the bright, warm castle, with its music and free-flowing champagne. She ran for safety. *Ran for her life.* Toward her family and her new husband and the crowds of beautiful, laughing, celebrating Swedes.

But the stranger caught up with her. She felt his hands roughly grab her and she screamed.

With a savage growl, he seized her, lifting her up in his arms, holding her tightly against his chest as if she weighed nothing at all. Her white, translucent veil flew behind them as he carried her across the snowy garden.

"What are you doing? Stop!" she cried, kicking and

struggling in his arms. "Let me go! Help! Someone help me!"

But no one came. No one could hear her screams inside the castle, over the noise of the orchestra.

Holding her, the man grimly waded through the snow toward the three black SUVs parked in the dark courtyard. She heard the three engines start. She screamed and twisted against him, fighting with all her strength, but her abductor barely seemed to notice.

And why should he? What was Rose's strength, compared to his?

He pushed her inside the back door of the last SUV, then slid in beside her, closing the door behind them.

"Go," he said.

The driver stomped on the gas, scattering rocks and gravel as the back tires slid on a patch of ice. The other two cars roared ahead of them, as they sped into the dark forested mountains of the countryside.

The dark stranger released Rose's wrist, glowering down at her.

Rubbing her wrist, she turned to look through the back window in time to see the castle disappear behind her. Her family, her new husband, everything that was rational and civilized and known—*gone*.

With a choked gasp, Rose looked at the madman beside her, the dark stranger who'd just stolen her away from everyone she loved. "You kidnapped me," she whispered. "From my own wedding reception."

The man stared back at her with dead eyes. His jaw clenched.

She moved away from him to the edge of her seat, her body pressing against the far door, her white tulle skirts spread all around her. "What do you want with me? Why have you taken me?"

The man's lips curved into a sinister smile as he leaned against the seat. His dark eyes bored into her soul with malevolence and dislike.

Then he reached for her. For a single moment she thought he meant to strike her, so she flinched, closing her eyes. Instead, she felt the tiara and veil ripped from her hair.

Her eyes flew open and she saw his window rolling down as he gripped her diamond tiara and the white gauzy veil in one hand.

"What are you doing?" she gasped.

He didn't reply. He just flung the tiara and veil out onto the road. The window slid noiselessly back up.

Rose stared out the back window. For an instant, she saw the diamonds sparkle and ghostly white veil wave across the snow behind them like a flag of surrender in a sliver of moonlight.

Then the SUV turned a corner, and it was gone.

Rose turned back, shaking in new fury. "How dare you?"

"It was a fake," the man replied coldly.

"It's a priceless heirloom. It has belonged to my husband's family for generations—"

"Fake," he cut her off. He turned away, adding in a low voice, "As fake as your so-called marriage."

"What?" she whispered.

"You heard me."

"You're mad."

For a moment she thought he wouldn't answer that,

either. Then his jaw twitched. "You know your marriage is fake. Just as you know who I am."

"I don't!"

"My name is Xerxes Novros," he bit out, watching her.

Xerxes Novros.

She'd heard Lars shouting out the name in a rage in a Swedish diatribe to his assistants and bodyguards. Now her husband's apparent enemy had kidnapped her.

Xerxes Novros.

Rose suddenly couldn't breathe. That name meant this wasn't a mistake. This wasn't a dream. She'd been kidnapped by her husband's enemy. And from what she'd seen, he was a remorseless, vicious villain with a heart of ice.

"What are you going to do with me?" she whispered.

Xerxes gave her a chilling smile. "Nothing. Absolutely nothing."

She didn't believe him for an instant. She had to get out of here, before he tossed *her* out the window next! She grabbed at her door handle, but it was locked.

Grimly, he shackled her wrists with his hands, pushing her back against the seat, his body crushing hers. "You cannot escape."

"Help!" she screamed, though she knew it was hopeless. "Somebody help me!"

"No help is coming for you, Rose Linden." He looked down at her with hatred in his black eyes. "You…are *mine*."

CHAPTER TWO

HE HADN'T expected her to be so beautiful.

As the SUV flew down the road through the snowy night, Xerxes Novros stared down at the petite blonde beneath him, her slender wrists shackled in his hands. The instant she'd tried to escape, he'd instinctively covered her with his body, pressing her into the soft leather of the backseat.

Xerxes could hear the soft pleading pant of her breath, smell the scent of fresh linen and tea roses that clung to her skin. Her every gasp lifted her full breasts higher above the tightly corseted satin bodice, until he thought the fabric could not contain her for much longer.

His body tightened, and he forced himself to look away.

He wasn't supposed to want Rose Linden. Despise her, yes. Use her? Certainly.

So how to explain this sudden rush of desire?

Xerxes generally had one requirement before he bedded a woman: he had to want her. That was it. He had no interest in learning about her character, her so-called *soul*. What would be the purpose of such an exercise? He'd be done with her by morning.

It wasn't as if his mistresses were innocent virgins.

They could take care of themselves. They had agendas of their own, usually lusting for his body, his money, his power or all three. Anyone could be bought, he knew. Everyone had a price.

But wanting *this* particular woman was a new low, even for him. Rose Linden was amoral and mercenary, devious and ruthless and cunning. He'd known that, but somehow, he hadn't expected her to be so beautiful. Now, he could almost understand why Lars Växborg had risked so much to take her as his pretend wife.

Any man would want to possess a woman like this.

She looked up at him, still panting, her eyes flashing. Her honey-blond hair had tumbled loose from the elegantly smooth chignon when he'd ripped the tiara off her head. Long blond tendrils now fell against her heart-shaped face, against skin like cream, smooth and fine with bright roses in her cheeks. Her eyes were the vivid turquoise of the Aegean, edged with thick black lashes. Her lips were full and pink and parted—her face flushed with passion and fury.

She looked, Xerxes thought, like a woman who'd just made love in the heat of explosive fire.

He wanted her. And that made him angry.

She must be luring him deliberately, he thought, teasing him like a coquette. Turning her feminine charms on him in hopes of evading punishment, in hope of winning his heart to her side.

Too bad for her that he had no heart.

His men had been watching Trollshelm Castle for days, since Xerxes had first heard about this so-called *wedding*. Xerxes had planned to kidnap the baron, and make him reveal Laetitia's location by force. But Lars

Växborg was too cagey for that. He'd never come out of his castle alone.

Xerxes couldn't wait any longer. After a year, he was no longer sure of Laetitia's condition. She could be dying. In desperation, he had nearly stormed into the castle with all his men, guns blazing, even knowing it could only end in disaster.

Then he'd seen the man's new bride leave the castle in the dark, moonlit garden. When Xerxes saw her illuminated by the eerie northern lights, he'd known it for the miracle it was. And he'd seized the opportunity.

Xerxes knew all about Rose Linden, the American waitress who squandered Laetitia's fortune on jewels and furs and designer clothes. The little gold digger had just lied her way through the most sacred vows of a marriage ceremony in order to become a rich baroness in the eyes of the world. Rather than escape her poverty through hard work, she had lied for it.

That was all Xerxes needed to know. He felt no pity. He felt nothing for her except scorn and cold anger.

Except that was no longer true. He now also felt lust.

Holding her down in the backseat of his Rolls-Royce, as he gripped her wrists in his hands and heard the pant of her breath, he hated her. *And he desired her.*

"You won't get away with this," she gasped.

"No?" He had to force himself to stay focused only on her eyes and not on her breasts, which were rising and falling rapidly with every breath. He gritted his teeth, focusing his gaze only on her face by an act of pure will.

"My husband will—"

"You have no husband."

"Oh, my God," she whimpered, growing still with shock and horror. "What have you done?"

"You know what I mean," he said grimly.

Her face grew white, her body absolutely motionless.

"Did you—did you hurt him?"

He'd been tempted to do just that, as recently as an hour ago; but killing Växborg, while personally satisfying, would have had negative repercussions. Xerxes could hardly take care of Laetitia from a jail cell. Especially since he could tell no one about their connection after he'd given his word.

"Take me back," Rose Linden whispered. "And I—I promise I'll never tell anyone what you did. I promise!"

"You *promise*?" he said scornfully. "We both know your *promise* is worthless."

"How can you say that?" Her voice trembled, choked with tears. "You don't even know me!"

Manufactured tears, he told himself, created by a cunning little actress. "I know enough," he replied harshly. "And now you and your lover will both pay—"

But at that, she began to struggle wildly, kicking at him with her high-heeled shoes. Her wide skirts flew over the backseat in waves of white lace and tulle. The driver in front nearly spun off the road as her knee hit the back of the seat. She kicked the window so hard that Xerxes had to grab her ankle to keep her from breaking the glass.

"Stop!" he commanded, using his body to compel her to obey. But to his amazement, though she was so much smaller, even though she had no chance of winning, she continued to fight.

"You bastard! You coward! You criminal!" she panted. "My husband will find you. He'll stop you. You'll never get away with this!"

All of her struggling only increased his desire for her. As she writhed beneath him, and he saw the spark of furious challenge in her eyes, the intensity of his need hit him like a wave. But why did she fight him, when it had to be clear that she had no chance of winning—that she'd already lost?

"Be still!" he demanded.

She stopped struggling, staring at him with dark rage, glaring her hatred and defiance. But it sparked a response in him that was even worse than lust. It was the last thing he wanted to feel for her.

A grudging respect.

As the convoy slowed down, he abruptly released her. Ahead in the moonlight, his largest jet was waiting for them on a deserted landing strip. Amid the whirl of softly shimmering snowflakes lifted from the ground by the wind, the runway had been swept clear of snow and looked like a black river, as dark as the sky above.

When Rose saw the jet, her whole body sagged with sudden despair. The SUV stopped, and she turned to him. A single tear streamed slowly down her cheek.

"Don't do this," she whispered. "Please...whatever quarrel you have with Lars, don't force me on that plane. Please, whoever you are—let me go back to the people I love!"

Love. As if this venal woman knew anything about love!

"Let me go back to my husband," she continued tearfully.

Xerxes's lip curled. "I told you. You have no husband."

She gasped, looking terrified.

He stared back at her as the driver opened his door. She knew perfectly well what he meant. It was an act. It had to be!

"I'm begging you," she whimpered, her blue eyes luminous with the light of unshed tears. "Don't hurt him!"

Roughly, he grabbed her arm.

"And the reason you have no husband," he bit out, "is because Lars Växborg already has a wife."

CHAPTER THREE

ROSE went numb with shock. As Xerxes pulled her from the SUV, leading her across the dark tarmac to the waiting plane, she did not resist.

"But he can't have a wife," she said numbly, looking up at him with bewildered confusion. "I'm Lars's wife!"

"The wedding was fake," he said coldly. "The vows were fake. The minister was fake. And most of all, Miss Linden—" he glanced down at her with glittering dark eyes as they reached the bottom of the steps "—*you* are fake."

He pushed her up the stairs into the cabin of the plane, where they were greeted by two flight attendants, the captain and the copilot. Bodyguards poured in behind them before they disappeared into the back of the jet.

The captain gave Xerxes a respectful nod. "We are ready for takeoff at your order, sir."

A brunette flight attendant took Xerxes's coat, while the other one, a redhead, greeted him with a silver tray holding drinks. Rose heard the cabin door close behind her with a loud bang.

"Thank you." Taking a flute of champagne from the tray, Xerxes sat down on a white leather seat in the front cabin of the jet. He turned carelessly back to Rose. "Champagne, Miss Linden? No?"

When Rose just stared at him in shock without replying, Xerxes gave a small, private smile and nodded at the captain. "You may proceed."

The captain and copilot disappeared to the front of the cabin to complete their takeoff preparations, and the flight attendants left for the back of the plane. Alone with Rose in the front cabin, Xerxes stretched out his arm on the back of the white leather seat. As he took a sip of his champagne, he seemed relaxed. *Contented.*

Rose stared at the crystal flute in that large, rough hand. Just an hour ago, she herself had been sipping champagne in the gilded ballroom of her husband's castle at her gorgeous wedding reception. Lars had looked up and smiled at her across the crowd.

Was it possible it had all been a lie?

A crack of pain went through her heart. No. It couldn't be true. Couldn't!

"You're wrong about Lars," Rose choked out. "He wouldn't have done this awful thing you're accusing him of—"

"Bigamy."

She flinched. "Don't use that horrible word!"

"You're right," he said coolly, finishing off his flute of champagne and setting it down. "It wasn't bigamy, because his wedding to you was a sham from start to finish."

"You're wrong!"

"Did you ever sign any paperwork?"

Rose sucked in her breath as she realized for the first

time that she'd never signed any papers. No marriage license. No forms. *Nothing.*

He watched her. "Växborg hasn't visited Sweden for years. None of his friends here know about his first marriage. But the minister who conducted your ceremony was an out-of-work actor from Stockholm."

"No," she said automatically. But she remembered how the minister had been strangely young and handsome. She'd been so nervous, almost sick, as she stood in the ruined shell of the ancient stone church and waited to speak her vows. She'd shrugged off the minister's soap-opera-star good looks, deciding all Swedish men must be as blond and handsome as Lars. But was it possible that what Xerxes Novros was telling her held some shred of truth…?

No! Rose shook her head fiercely. "Lars wouldn't have pursued me if he were already married. He wouldn't have even noticed me pouring his coffee in San Francisco!"

"He wouldn't?"

"No! He wouldn't! Marriage lasts forever. It is the friendship and passion that lasts your whole life. Loyalty and love are the foundation of everything!"

He stared at her sardonically. "And where did you hear that, princess?"

"I didn't have to *hear* it from anyone," she snapped. "My parents have been married for nearly forty years. My grandparents were married for sixty before my granddad died. All my brothers and sisters are married except for one. All married. Happily. Forever."

Xerxes looked at her for a long time, then pressed the intercom. When the flight attendant came through the door, he turned to her, pushing the empty champagne flute back into her hands. His voice was almost surly as he said, "Scotch. Rocks."

As she left, Xerxes turned back to Rose. "I can see marriage means a great deal to you." He gave a hard look at the ostentatious diamond on her left hand. "So much that you didn't mind speaking a few false vows in order to get your hands on *that*."

He thought she cared about this huge diamond ring? She clasped her hands together tightly. Rose didn't care about jewelry, only what it symbolized! "You think I would have let Lars even flirt with me if I'd thought he was married? Never!"

"Everything is for sale in this world. Everyone has a price. And clearly—" he looked with scorn from her ring to her designer wedding gown "—that was yours."

"The lace was hand-stitched by nuns in France," Lars had told her proudly when he'd presented it to her. He'd laughed at Rose's desire to wear her mother's simple 1960s-era wedding gown to a simple ceremony in her California hometown. *"I will plan everything, petal. All you will need to do is be beautiful—and be ready for our honeymoon!"*

Shaking the memory from her mind, Rose took a steadying breath.

"You're wrong," she said. "Either you've made a mistake, or...or..."

Or you're lying, she wanted to say, but didn't have the courage, faced with his wrathful gaze.

Rising to his feet, her captor crossed two steps to her. His eyes were like black fire. He towered over her, and she had to force herself not to cower, but to stand straight and tall, to stand her ground.

"Växborg has no money of his own. His money comes from his wife's inheritance, from her wealthy mother." His lips twisted as he scornfully touched the exquisite lace of her sleeve. "That's her money you're wearing on your back right now."

"I don't believe you."

"Keep on telling yourself that, princess."

"If any of this were true, if he were as bad as you say, why wouldn't his wife just divorce him?"

Xerxes looked away, his jaw clenching. "She can't."

"Why?"

Narrowing his eyes, he looked at her. "They were in an accident. She's in a coma. Not that you would care."

His tone made it clear he thought Rose was a greedy, heartless brat. She—who'd worked two jobs to pay her own way through college, to help her parents survive since the family business went bankrupt!

Rose blinked fast. At that moment, the engine grew louder as the jet started to move down the runway. She nearly stumbled as it jolted forward.

"Sit down," he said.

Ignoring the lump in her throat, she braced her arm against the ceiling and lifted her chin. "Don't you dare tell me—"

"Sit down," he barked.

Her knees failed beneath her and she fell onto the white leather couch with a *whomp*. She realized to her shock that her body had obeyed him, even when her mind had refused.

The plane accelerated down the runway as he sat beside her. She gripped the armrest. He calmly reached for his laptop.

Once they were airborne, Rose glanced out the tiny window. All she could see was endless darkness with eerie moonlit clouds.

No one could help her now. She was on her own. She took several deep breaths, trying to keep herself from panicking. "Where are you taking me?"

He didn't answer. He stared at the screen on his laptop and typed rapidly, then took a sip of the Scotch that the smiling stewardess brought him on a tray. Rose waited until they were left alone again before she spoke.

"Where are you taking me?" she repeated more forcefully.

"It's irrelevant."

"Tell me where."

"I hardly think you're in a position to make demands."

"You kidnapped me!"

"Such a melodramatic word."

"How else would you describe it?"

"Justice," he said coldly.

"You don't have my passport."

"That's all been arranged."

"How?"

He shrugged. "As everything else is. For a price."

Watching beads of water condense on the outside of his glass tumbler, she clenched her hands into fists.

"Tell me where we're going *right now*," she raged. "Or else…or else…"

He looked at her, his dark eyes amused. "Or else?"

Oh, how she wished she had her brother's old baseball bat, or even a heavy handbag to threaten him with! She tried to look very mean as she thundered, "You will tell me where we're going or I will make this flight your own private hell!"

Xerxes stared at her for a long instant. "Now that I believe," he said mildly as his lips quirked. Typing a few last words on his computer, he turned back to face her and said, "I am taking you to Greece."

"Why?"

"To force Växborg to give me what I want."

"And that is?"

"If he *loves* you like you think," he said the word scornfully, "he will agree to a trade."

"Trade?" She stared at him. "What trade?"

"You. For her." Taking another sip of Scotch, he set the tumbler down on the table and looked at her evenly. "I will use you to force him to divorce his wife. His real wife."

Rose stared at him. Slowly, she lifted her chin.

"I am his real wife," she said quietly. "And nothing you can say will convince me otherwise."

Xerxes frowned. "Is it really possible—" he searched her gaze with narrowed eyes "—that you did not know?"

She shook her head. "There is nothing to know! You've made a horrible mistake!"

"I couldn't understand why he would pretend to marry you like this. But if you didn't know he already had a wife…" His eyes traced her face, her breasts, her body. He tilted his head curiously. "Did you give him some kind of ultimatum? Did he think pretending to marry you was the only way he could keep you in his bed?"

To *keep* her in Lars's bed? Rose gaped at him. She'd never been in his bed—or any man's! She was saving her virginity for her wedding night!

The thought made her suck in her breath.

Surely Lars wouldn't have gone through such an elaborate wedding pretense just to get her into his bed…?

"I will do anything for you," Lars had said urgently last week, his pale blue eyes boring into hers. *"Anything, petal. This is torture. You must be mine."*

With a ragged breath, Rose pushed the memory aside. "Our marriage was real," she said. "There is no other wife."

Abruptly, Xerxes moved to the chair directly across from her. He leaned forward, and the knees of his long legs brushed the wide skirts of her wedding gown.

"I am telling you the truth, Rose," he said quietly.

She stared up at him. His face was too brutally masculine to be conventionally handsome like Lars's sleek blond features. Instead, Xerxes had a hard, square jawline that was already dark with shadow. He had an aquiline nose and dark eyebrows above black eyes as endless and luminous as the night. His hair was cut short, above his ear, but with a slightly mussed, wild wave.

As he leaned forward, looking into her eyes, she was aware of the warmth and strength of his body. Against her will, she was suddenly aware of the rhythm of his breath, deep and in time with hers. She was aware of his scent, the masculine combination of some kind of woodsy cologne and musk and leather.

He was so close to her. So close.

With a ragged breath, she looked away.

"Who is she, then?" Rose said in a small voice. "His supposed first wife?"

"Laetitia Van Reyn."

"Van Reyn?"

"You know the name?"

"There's a wealthy family in San Francisco, mentioned often in the newspapers..."

"The same," he said grimly.

"But the parents are dead," Rose recalled. "Their only child is barely out of high school. I read she left for college."

"She's in a coma," he said brutally. "No one knows she needs help. And I can't find her and get her to a hospital." His black gaze traced over her. "But you are his weakness. He will trade her. For you."

She shook her head, dazed.

"You are the most beautiful woman I've ever seen. Except for...that." He frowned as his eyes narrowed. "Take that off."

"What?"

"Your dress. Take it off."

"What are you talking about?"

"The wedding dress is an insult. To her. To me. Take it off. You are not a bride."

"I was—am!"

"Take off that dress," he growled. "Or I will take it off for you."

"I have nothing else to wear!"

He gave her a cold smile. "That is not my problem."

She rose to her feet in fury, lifting her chin. "I have the right to wear this. I am a bride, a married woman. You're a liar!"

He swiftly rose to his feet, like a predator. "Call me that again, princess," he said dangerously.

"Baroness," she corrected fiercely. She tossed her hair, glaring up at him with all the fury of her five feet, four inches. Her eyes glittered as she met him toe to toe. "And you, Xerxes Novros, are a *liar!*"

CHAPTER FOUR

"YOU'RE a liar!"

Young and dark-haired, Laetitia Van Reyn had gripped the gilded arms of her chair as she stared at Xerxes in her family's mansion with views of the Golden Gate Bridge. She'd remained home from boarding school after her father's death to support her fragile mother, who had collapsed at his funeral. *"No!"* Laetitia had jumped to her feet at Xerxes's news. Her hands flew to her ears as she backed away. *"You're a liar! Get out of my house! Never come back!"*

Xerxes blinked. Liar. Same accusation. Very different woman.

He stared now at the young blonde who stood before him in the cabin of his private jet. Rose Linden was magnificent. A little too thin, perhaps, but it was hard to notice that when her full breasts swelled up against the bodice with every angry breath. Her waist was tiny, the perfect span for a man's hands. Her honey-blond hair fell back in waves as she tossed her head, her chignon now completely collapsed, exposing her swanlike throat. Her aquamarine eyes glittered at him in fury.

"You are a liar," Rose cried. "I don't believe a word you say!"

A liar. To Xerxes, the integrity of a man's promise equaled his worth as a man. It was the one accusation he could not endure. In cold rage, he gripped her shoulders.

"I'm selfish," he ground out. "Ruthless. Even cruel. But not a liar. Never that."

His gaze fell to her mouth, where she was chewing on her lower lip. He saw her lick her lips with her wet pink tongue, and his body tightened.

He wanted her. And in this moment, the layers of her wedding dress were all that separated them.

The wedding dress.

She was continuing to defiantly wear it, as a visual, physical insult both to Xerxes and to Växborg's real wife. As if Laetitia were already forgotten. As if she were already dead!

Xerxes's hands slowly moved down her arms, against the see-through lace of her sleeves. His lips turned down grimly.

"I told you to take that dress off."

He felt her shiver, even as she stuck out her chin and glared at him with her beautiful turquoise eyes.

"No."

"Then I will take it off for you."

Her eyes widened. "You wouldn't dare to—"

With a rough motion, he ripped apart the shoulders of her wedding dress, tearing through the layers of white lace and popping the line of tiny white buttons off the back. He yanked the sleeves down her arms with such force that she staggered forward, nearly falling to her knees.

He discarded the haute couture gown, with its

elaborate layers of white lace and tulle, to the floor of the airplane cabin. He started to press the intercom button to call one of the attendants for a robe. Then he froze.

Rose stood before him, the wedding dress crumpled like a tablecloth at her feet. All she wore was the white silk lingerie intended for her wedding night, a tiny white bra, lacy thong panties and white stockings attached with a garter belt.

He could not look away from the vision of her half-naked body, of her creamy skin and perfect curves. He gaped at the perfect hourglass shape of her petite body, at her full breasts and hips, at her tiny waist, and nearly gasped aloud.

Insult or not, he'd been a fool to take the wedding gown off of her. The image of her beauty was dangerous. *To him.*

He should have known she'd be wearing tarty white lingerie for her wedding night to the baron. Pretending to be a virgin—just *pretending*, because he'd obviously been bedding her for some time. No man would resist Rose's charms, her soft blond beauty, her lush body. They must have been lovers from the moment the man had plucked her from that restaurant in San Francisco.

Växborg was guilty. But was Rose? Had she known about Laetitia?

It doesn't matter, he told himself harshly. Whether or not Rose had known about his marriage, she'd been eager enough to marry the baron for the sake of his money, his title and his snakelike charm. Everyone had their price. Xerxes learned that long ago. Feelings were a commodity like everything else.

And yet Xerxes's eyes traced unwillingly over her beautiful, near-naked body.

Rose's cheeks were red as she looked down, breathing rapidly. She started to cover herself with her slender arms. Then she stopped, gripping her hands into fists at her sides. Slowly, she lifted her chin, her eyes glittering at him in fury.

What a woman, he thought in amazement. Even now, completely in his power, when any other woman might have been prostrate with fear, Rose defied him.

"You owe Lars a wedding dress now," she said in a low voice. "As well as a diamond tiara. And a bride."

With dignity, she bent to pick up the dress, then used the tattered remnants to cover herself.

Why did he want her like this? How could this mere girl, this waitress, have such an overwhelming effect on his body?

Setting his jaw, he reached for her. She looked up with an intake of breath, but instead of ripping the dress from her hands, he helped her cover herself with it. He slowly moved his fingers up her naked arms. Her skin was smooth and warm.

She looked up at him in bewilderment. Her lips parted. Her full, delectable pink lips, so ripe for a man's plunder.

Suddenly, Xerxes knew what he had to do. He knew just the way to learn the truth about her innocence or guilt.

He would kiss her.

If she were truly the heartless gold digger he'd first believed, she would not only allow his kiss, she would try to lure him into a full-scale seduction. To evade punishment, she would change allegiance, wanting to win him over to her side.

If not…

Well. Xerxes would put her to the test.

The fact that he could think of nothing but kissing her had nothing to do with this. It was a scientific experiment. Satiating his desire would be just a fortunate bonus.

After he'd replaced the torn dress over her shoulders, Rose gripped the gaping front bodice together with her hand and glared as him with hostility.

"Don't think that you can bully me into being afraid of you, because I will never—"

Her words ended in a gasp as Xerxes seized her in his arms. Lowering his mouth to hers, he brutally kissed her.

CHAPTER FIVE

His lips were hard and hot against hers, overwhelming Rose's senses in a ruthless assault.

She stiffened, pressing her hands instinctively against his chest. He leaned her back, deepening the kiss, forcibly pressing her lips apart. As he plundered her mouth with his tongue, she felt a shock of sudden pleasure so sharp and raw that she gasped. As his lips moved against hers, forcing her to respond, she was swept beneath the waves of sensation. He held her tightly and she felt the world swirl and twist around them, lost in a spinning current of desire she'd never experienced before.

She tasted the sweetness of his breath, the taste of Scotch on his tongue. She felt the roughness of his jaw against her skin, the heat of him against her body.

Overpowered by her captor's strength and the intensity of his commanding embrace, she surrendered. She'd never been kissed before, truly kissed, and her brain shut off abruptly. She was briefly lost in the stroking touch of his fingers against her bare back, in the feeling of his muscular thighs straining against hers. He held her in his strong arms, keeping her from falling to the floor.

Without her mind's permission, her lips moved against his. She had no idea what she was doing, but pleasure such as she'd never felt before ripped through her body with sweet agony, making her tremble and shake. She reached her arms around his neck, as if to pull him closer, as if she knew that he and only he could provide the air she needed to breathe....

Then she realized what she was doing. With a choked gasp, she ripped herself away from him. Staring up at him in horror, she sucked in her breath.

Drawing back her hand, she slapped his face.

Xerxes stared at her with surprise, his hand on his reddening cheek.

"How dare you kiss me!" she shouted, her hand still throbbing with pain from the strength of her blow. "I am a married woman!"

His lips twisted lazily as he suddenly relaxed. "You are not," he said calmly, lifting a dark eyebrow. "And I weary of this discussion. But I'm finished. The kiss was merely to obtain the answer to a question."

Which made no sense at all! "What question?"

He shrugged. "You did not know Växborg was married, or you would have tried to seduce me, to win me to your side. Which, with that clumsy kiss, you assuredly did not."

Clumsy? Her cheeks became red as she sucked in her breath. She was clumsy?

It had been her first kiss. As a teenager, she'd been determined to wait for her idealistic vision of love's first kiss; later, in her twenties, she'd felt too awkward to force it. A twenty-nine-year-old virgin was bad enough, but a woman that age who'd never even been kissed?

She had absolutely no intention of explaining that

to Xerxes Novros, however, leaving herself open to his mockery!

"I see now that you're not guilty of any crime," he said carelessly, "except being gullible and naive."

Gullible and naive. Rose stared at him. Well, maybe she was. Her lips still felt bruised where he'd kissed her. What was wrong with her? How could she have kissed him back, even for an instant? How could she have let her body utterly overrule her brain—and her heart?

"Don't touch me again."

"I won't."

Swallowing, she looked away. The electricity that had coursed through her body when he'd kissed her had been nothing like she'd ever felt before. She'd certainly never felt that way with Lars, not even when she'd allowed him to give her a single brief peck as the minister pronounced them man and wife!

She hated her captor, but not half so much as she hated herself at that moment.

"I mean it. If you try to kiss me again," she said in a low voice, "I will kill you."

"You are threatening me?" He sounded amused.

"Yes," she snapped. It was no doubt stupid to threaten to kill a ruthless millionaire while trapped on his jet, but she was so angry and humiliated—and so overwhelmed still by the force of his kiss, the kiss he'd called *clumsy*—that she was beyond good sense.

His lips twisted into an amused half smile as he considered her. "All right."

"All...all right?"

"I won't kiss you again."

She frowned, wondering if it was a trick. "You won't?"

"I give you my word," he said carelessly. "I won't kiss you again. Not unless you beg me."

"Perfect," she said, wrapping her arms around her shivering body. "Because I will never, ever ask you to kiss me."

Turning away, he sat down and reached for the tumbler, finishing the Scotch in one easy swallow. "Now that we have that settled..." He pressed the intercom. When a flight attendant entered, he told her abruptly, "Miss Linden is tired. Escort her to the bedroom."

Rose whirled on him. "Your bedroom! I should have known it was a trick—"

"I will stay here," he interrupted. He gave Rose one last glance with his inscrutable black eyes. "You have nothing to be afraid of now. Go rest. We will land in a few hours."

Tucked in a tiny private bedroom at the back of the plane, Rose spent the remainder of the flight sitting in a hard chair beside the window, clutching her tattered wedding dress to her chest beneath a blanket, and staring out at the dark night.

Remembering the dark power of his embrace was like fire through her limbs. She still felt the hard heat of his mouth against hers, forcing her lips apart as he took her at his will.

The shock of pleasure had been beyond words. Beyond reason. And she hated him for it.

She stared out the tiny round window into the darkness. She tried to think of something else. Was her family terrified, waiting anxiously for news of her? Was

Lars weeping, combing the bottom of his moat for her drowned body?

Please, let him have called the police, she prayed. Closing her eyes, she hoped feverishly that when they landed in Greece, they'd be met by a whole squadron who would cart Xerxes Novros off to prison like he deserved! Curling up in the chair, she imagined progressively more painful punishments for her kidnapper, until she must have fallen asleep to the enjoyable dreams before she felt his hand shaking her awake.

Her eyes flew open. Disoriented, she sat up.

Xerxes stood before her by the bed. She saw the plane had landed. Outside, the night was still dark, she saw a small, desolate airstrip by the sea. No flashing lights. No policemen.

Disappointment flashed through her.

Narrowing her eyes, she looked away. "I'm not leaving this jet."

Xerxes held out his hand. "You will be far more comfortable in the house."

She folded her arms coolly. "I'll stay here, thank you."

"Don't you wish to speak with your boyfriend on the phone?"

His use of the word *boyfriend* made her fury spark. "You mean my *husband*."

He snorted. "You are a stubborn woman."

She rubbed her eyes wearily. Just thinking about how worried her family must all be about her made her need that phone call more than anything on earth. She glared up at her captor.

"Do you give your word that you do not intend to harm me?"

He curled his lip. "I would never hurt a woman." He rubbed his cheek ruefully.

"A captive has the right to defend herself," she said stiffly.

He looked down at her. "I would expect no less of you."

He wasn't staring at her with that hot light of hatred anymore. And yet there was still an undercurrent between them that she didn't understand.

She missed Lars, who was so charmingly predictable, who though he didn't always listen to her words, always gave her endless compliments. It had made her feel a bit uncomfortable, actually, the way he always stared at her so hungrily, telling her over and over that she was perfect. She knew she wasn't perfect. But she'd told herself he had many years to understand her better after she became his wife.

If she even *was* his wife.

No! Rose pushed away the gnawing fear growing inside her. She couldn't—wouldn't—allow Xerxes to make her doubt Lars! She couldn't trust this brutal, powerful man who'd kidnapped her, her husband's enemy who'd just kissed her against her will.

Xerxes's words were lies. *They had to be.*

She would have faith. Lars would save her and prove she was his true and legal wife. She wouldn't allow Xerxes to make her doubt everything she believed in—not even for an instant!

Slowly, she rose to her feet, holding the torn bodice

of her wedding gown tightly together over her chest. "As long as I have your word you won't harm me."

He gently brushed hair from her cheek. Lowering his head, he whispered in her ear, "I will not harm you."

He drew back, looking down at her. Then he held out his hand, steady and strong and confident.

She stared at it. Then, not touching him, she brushed past him regally, as if she still wore a tiara on her head. A baroness in exile.

Her gown still covered her body decently well, as long as she held together the bodice at the jagged, gaping rip over her heart. But she had to hold it tightly. The tulle skirts were heavy and wide, pulling behind her like a train as she went down the steps to the tarmac.

Several cars were waiting, including a black Bentley. As she approached, a uniformed driver opened the passenger door.

"If you please," Xerxes said quietly, pressing his hand gently against her back. She shivered at his touch, then jumped forward as if he'd burned her.

Silently, he followed her.

The black car drove through the dark night along the edge of a coastal road. She looked out and saw moonlight shimmering across black water. Strange, she thought, to think it was that exact same moonlight shining down on Trollshelm Castle right now.

"Are we near Athens?" she asked to break the silence.

"On an island in the Aegean."

"Which island?"

"Mine."

Shocked, she turned to face him. "*Your* island?"

He shrugged.

"You own the whole island?"

"I own several."

Her mouth fell open. "Why on earth would you own *several* islands? Or even one, for that matter!"

"I loan the others out to friends who want to relax without the glare of media attention."

"So your friends can be alone with their mistresses or something?"

He shrugged.

Grinding her teeth, Rose folded her arms. What else would she expect from a man completely without morals? "How many islands do you have? Or have you lost count?"

"Three now. I recently sold the fourth in exchange for a palace in Istanbul."

A palace in Istanbul?

"Oh," she said faintly, trying to act as if that were a normal sort of trade.

"Officially," he amended, "our trade was an office building in Paris for a few hundred million euros." He shrugged. "The palace, and then the island, were just tossed in later as extras."

"Right. Extras." She swallowed, thinking of her own recent trade of a box of homemade chocolates to an upstairs neighbor in her apartment building in exchange for a macaroni-and-cheese casserole. "Um. Your friend must have really wanted a private place to hide his mistress."

Xerxes snorted. "I wouldn't exactly call Rafael Cruz a *friend*." He looked away and added softly, "Anyway, I was glad to be rid of that island."

"Sure." Rose held up her hand airily. "Owning private Greek islands gets so very dull. I've sold all mine recently for Japanese tea houses."

His lips quirked, then he shook his head. "I grew up on that particular island. My grandfather was a fisherman. Even after my grandparents were dead and I replaced the old shack with a villa, I never wanted to go back there."

Xerxes had once been poor? For a moment, sympathy threatened to prey on Rose, weakening her. Then she hardened her heart and glared at him.

"It sucks to be you," she said acidly. "Owning too many private islands, forced to travel all over the world in your jet. Kidnapping married women. You're clearly a hard case." She glanced out the car window. "So why are we here and not at your shiny new Turkish palace?"

He turned to look out the window, blocking her view of his face. "I brought you here because this is my home."

Rose's jaw dropped.

"You brought me to your *home*? But, but…" She faltered, then said, "Lars will know exactly where to find you!"

He turned back to her. "Exactly."

"I don't understand. What kind of kidnapping is this?"

"I told you. It's not a kidnapping. It's a trade."

The car stopped and the driver opened the door. Xerxes climbed out, then held out his hand back to her.

Careful not to touch his hand, she tripped and stumbled out of the car. She glanced back at him, blushing.

He pulled back his hand, tucking it behind his back.

"Come," he said, regaining his low, mocking voice. "I'm sure you're eager to see the inside of your prison. Baroness."

But he didn't try to touch her again. She was relieved. After his electric kiss earlier, after feeling the strength of his body and the heat of his embrace that had made her surrender against her will, she was afraid to let him so much as brush his fingertip against her skin.

Following him toward the house, she looked up. Her footsteps faltered.

She'd once dreamed of traveling to Greece, but she'd never imagined anything like this.

The enormous white villa sat on the edge of a sharp cliff, iced with moonlight. The cold, classical architecture made it look like a fortress, and suddenly reminded her of another island closer to home. The prison of Alcatraz.

She caught up with him inside the tall doorway. She only dimly saw the servants awaiting them, greeting Xerxes in low, respectful voices before they disappeared down dark hallways.

He pulled her into a high-ceilinged library edged with leather-bound books. When he opened the French doors to the veranda, a cool breeze blew off the sea, curling up her spine. Rose shivered.

Xerxes turned back to her. "Are you hungry?"

"No," she whispered, then closed her eyes, trying not to cry. "I just want to call my family."

"Your family?" he queried, his lips curving sardonically. "Not your precious boyfriend?"

She blinked. She'd actually forgotten about Lars for a

moment. But it was only natural, she told herself. She'd known Lars only a few months, while she'd loved her family for her whole life! But still, the thought brought her up short. Shouldn't she have wanted to speak to Lars above all others?

Pushing the disquieting thought aside, she glared at him. "My husband *is* my family."

Xerxes pulled out his phone, dialed a number and handed it to her. "Here."

She stared up at him in surprise, her mouth gaping as she held the phone in her hand. "Is this a trick?"

"It's ringing," he pointed out.

With a gasp, she pushed the phone to her ear. When she heard Lars's voice at the other end, she nearly wept with relief. "Lars!"

"Rose?" he said, his voice more high-pitched that usual. "Where are you? One of my groundskeepers found the tiara smashed in the road. Your family is worried sick. Why did you leave?" His voice wavered. "Did you hear something that made you angry? Whatever it was, I can explain—"

"I've been kidnapped," she sobbed. "I'm in Greece."

There was silence on the other end. Then Lars spoke grimly.

"Novros," he said. "Novros took you, didn't he?"

How had he known that?

"Yes," she choked out. "And he—"

"What did he tell you?"

She turned away so Xerxes couldn't see her tearful face as she whispered into the phone, "He's told me all kinds of lies. Oh, Lars. He said you were already married, that the tiara was fake, that our *wedding* was fake! Ridiculous lies that no one would believe!"

Sniffling, she waited for Lars to tell her that of course it was a lie, that of course she was his legal wife and that he'd be calling Interpol immediately.

Instead, there was silence.

"It's complicated," he said weakly.

The word was a stab to her heart. "Complicated?"

"I pawned my grandmother's tiara a few years ago, but the glass version looks almost the same," he said defensively. "I intended to buy it back, but never got around to it. Your engagement ring is real though!"

Why was he talking about jewelry? Who cared about that? She choked out, "But the other things—"

"Well, technically I suppose you could say that I was already married, but my so-called wife has been comatose for a year. She's a vegetable. I never loved her, Rose, but I needed money, don't you understand? I have an image to uphold. And I swear to you," he said urgently, "Laetitia is nothing to me."

"You're married," Rose whispered numbly, feeling like she was in a nightmare. She felt Xerxes move behind her, felt the warmth emanating off his strong body. "Our wedding today was really fake."

"I had no choice. You wouldn't let me touch you!" Lars said. "I hired an actor to lead the vows. It was easy. None of my friends knew about Laetitia. The day after we eloped, my stupid, brainless wife drove her car into a telephone pole."

Rose sucked in her breath.

As if sensing he'd gone too far, Lars changed his tone. "You're the one I love, petal, my perfect bride. You are the one I truly want as my wife. I always intended to renew our vows, legally, as soon as Laetitia died. The doctors say she's fading fast," he added eagerly. "She could die any day."

"You…" Her throat closed. It took her a minute to force out the words. "You *want* her to die?"

"Of course I do!" he said. "I need you, my beautiful Rose. Please, petal, you have to believe…"

But Rose heard no more. The phone fell from her numb hands, clattering to the marble floor.

She stared dimly at the sparkling diamond ring on her hand. She'd pledged her faith to a man who was not free. And worse than that, a man devious enough to twist Rose's innocent words into the justification for his deception. A man heartless enough to want his comatose wife to die.

Rose had believed in him. She'd thought she'd truly married him. And in a few hours more, she would have given him her virginity.

How could she have been such a fool?

The entire fairy tale had been a lie.

Her knees collapsed. Peeling the diamond ring off her finger, she threw it across the room, where it ricocheted off the bookcase. Covering her face with her hands as she wept, she sank to the white marble floor.

Xerxes picked up the ring from the floor, along with the dropped phone. He put the phone to his ear.

"So," he said coolly. "Shall we trade?"

She dimly heard Lars's furious shouting in response.

"This is my last offer," Xerxes said carelessly. "I will allow you to keep your castle, even to keep the car you bought with her money. But you will give her up, along with the rest of her fortune. You will complete the divorce within the week. Or you will regret it."

More shouting.

Xerxes's gaze was dark as he looked down at Rose. "We both know you will agree. And Växborg? Do it as soon as you can. Your mistress is a beautiful woman." His lips curved into a cruel, sensual smile. "Any man would commit crimes to possess her."

CHAPTER SIX

AFTER he ended the call, the library was silent. Rose heard only low, soft snuffles that she realized were her own sobs.

Her captor stood over her, and she felt his silent, considering gaze upon her. She tried to stifle her weeping but could not.

All she could think about was that Xerxes had been right. Lars had betrayed her. Tricked her. He'd used her own idealistic nature, her belief in loyalty and love, against her.

He'd never loved Rose at all. He'd only wanted her body. He was already married, and he'd been waiting… waiting for…

"He's waiting for his wife to die," she whispered aloud.

She felt Xerxes touch her arm. "I know."

She looked up. His dark eyes were surprisingly gentle.

"Come," he said in a low voice. "You've had a rough day. I'll take you to bed."

She was unable to resist as he took her hand in his larger one, lifting her to her feet. She trembled at his touch, barely feeling strong enough to hold the bodice of her wedding gown closed with her other hand. She pressed her fingers against her heart. She felt faint, her knees weak as she tried to walk. Stopped.

She looked up at him in the dark, shadowy hallway. She saw the roughness in his expression. He was everything Lars was not: brutal, ruthless, vengeful. *Truthful*.

Abruptly, Xerxes lifted her into his strong arms, holding her against his chest. She felt the rush of electricity, the overwhelming awareness sizzling through her just as it had when he'd first touched her, when he'd kissed her on the plane.

He didn't know that it had been her first kiss. And that her whole body trembled now with all the desire and yearning of twenty-nine years of loneliness.

He carried her down the shadowed hallway and up a sweeping flight of stairs. The rhythm of his footsteps was heavy against the marble floor, mingling like percussion against the music of the roaring surf outside.

She glanced up at his face. His expression was brutal, even cruel. And yet he held her so gently. She'd thought him some kind of malevolent demon, but perhaps he wasn't. Perhaps he was a dark angel, who'd unexpectedly come to save her.

At the end of the hall, he used his shoulder to push open a door with a low creak. Supporting Rose's body with one arm as if she weighed nothing at all—which she probably did, compared to him—he switched on a small lamp with his free hand.

She dimly saw a large, Spartan bedroom, utterly masculine, devoid of color. The walls were white. The bed was black. The wide windows had a balcony overlooking the moonlit sea.

He set her down on the bed. Looking down at her, his eyes were dark as night. Dark—and full of hunger.

He was going to kiss her again. She knew it. He was going to kiss her, despite his promise. Promises meant nothing to men. They'd meant nothing to Lars. Now Xerxes would ruthlessly possess her. He would take everything she had once hoped to give her husband in innocence and faith.

Rose no longer had the strength to fight.

He pushed her back against the enormous bed. Slowly, he pulled the fabric of the bodice from her clenched fingers, leaving her silken bra and the bare skin of her belly in clear view. She felt the magnetic force of his body over her own, his powerful strength and size as he stared down at her, pinning her with his dark gaze.

She stared at him numbly. She had to fight. *Why couldn't she fight?* She breathed, "I...I hate you."

His sensual mouth curved as he looked down at her. "I don't need you to love me. I just need you to obey."

Rose closed her eyes, waiting for him to rip the wedding dress down her legs and throw his body over hers. Waiting for him to ravish her without hesitation, to ruthlessly and brutally seduce her naked body.

She almost didn't care. She'd lost herself completely. Just a few hours ago, she'd been idealistic, romantic. Now, she felt—nothing.

Then he touched her.

His fingertips were feather-light, running along her bare collarbone to her shoulder. Strange sensations coursed through her body, an odd tumble of emotions that frightened her. Fear? Yes. But also…something more than fear. Something greater than fear that made her tremble deep inside.

His hands moved slowly down the naked valley between her breasts, causing prickles to spread all over her body. His hands sizzled everywhere he touched. Her breasts felt heavy, her nipples tightening to aching points beneath the silky white bralette that Lars had insisted on ordering for her from Paris. She'd blushed when he'd given it to her. Now, she was wearing it in front of his enemy.

His fingers moved down her bare belly to the tattered wedding gown pulled down around her waist. He gently pulled the layers of lace and tulle down her legs, then dropped it to the floor in a crumpled heap.

"I knew I'd get that off you eventually," he whispered.

She started to reply, then saw that he'd fallen to his knees at the foot of the bed. The image of him kneeling before her half-naked body was so shocking that she squeezed her eyes shut.

But if anything, the sensation only grew more intense as she felt his hands on her thigh, unhooking a lace garter that held up her white silk stocking. The warmth of his breath curled against her naked belly, and she gasped with the sweet agony of forbidden desire. She shouldn't feel like this—not for a stranger!

He slowly pulled the stocking down her leg, his fingers brushing her skin from her thigh to her knee. The sensual silk slid slowly down her calf, down her ankle to the sensitive hollow of her foot. And suddenly her leg was bare.

He moved on the mattress, moving up between her legs. With a gasp, she opened her eyes.

He was looking down at her, his dark eyes hungry. Holding her gaze with his own, he tossed the stocking to the floor. Reaching for her other thigh, he unclasped the garter and moved the second stocking down her leg, sliding the silk down her skin like the whisper of a caress.

Heat built inside her, coursing through her body, sizzling her with his every look and every touch. Tension tightened her nipples to aching points, coiling low in her belly. Her breaths came in increasingly quick gasps.

She shouldn't do this. He was her captor, a criminal, a stranger to her! She shouldn't let him touch her!

But even as her mind screamed for her to push away, she couldn't move. She just lay there on the soft cotton sheets, feeling the breeze from the open window, seeing it wave through white translucent curtains. In the distance, she heard the plaintive call of seagulls and her own hoarse breath. Biting her lip until it bruised, she looked up at his brutal face.

But he did not look brutal anymore. He stroked her concave belly with concern. "So thin," he murmured. "Why so thin?"

It broke the spell. She sat up abruptly.

"Gullible. Clumsy. Skinny," Rose said bitterly, as her fingers gripped the cotton sheets, pulling them up. "You are cruel. Lars always said I was the most beautiful girl in the world—"

Then her throat choked as she remembered that Lars was a heartless, soulless liar.

Xerxes's fingers stilled. "Växborg did not lie," he

said quietly. "You are the most beautiful woman I've ever seen, Rose Linden."

He pushed her down firmly with his rough hands, and she did not resist. She closed her eyes. When she felt a soft sheet cover her body, she looked at him in shock.

From beside the bed, Xerxes looked down at her with a crooked smile. His rugged face was impossibly handsome in the circle of lamplight. He lifted a white goose-down comforter over the sheet. And suddenly, she realized what he was doing. He wasn't trying to seduce her.

He was tucking her in for the night.

"You're leaving me?" she whispered as he turned away. "Just like that?"

He paused at the door, his expression half-hidden by shadow. The dim golden light illuminated the edges of his muscular body as he spoke to her without turning around. "Good night."

"I don't understand. Why are you acting like this?"

"Like what?"

"Like a gentleman. Like…like a good person."

Abruptly, he clicked off the light, and the room fell into darkness. "Don't think I'm a good person," he said in a low voice. "If you do, you'll regret it. 'Til the day you die."

And he left, closing the door heavily behind him, locking her in—alone.

CHAPTER SEVEN

ROSE woke up the next morning to find sunshine flooding her with white, almost blinding clarity. It refreshed her, washing away the dark nightmares that had troubled her all night.

Yawning, she blinked sleepily. *It was a dream*, she thought. *Thank heaven it was all a dream.* She was back in her solitary bedroom at Trollshelm Castle. Today was her wedding day, the day she would pledge herself as Lars's wife for the rest of her life....

Rose blinked.

She sat up abruptly. Her blankets fell to her waist as she stared around her. *This was not her bedroom.*

She glanced down at the white silk bra and panties that she'd slept in. A blush heated her cheeks as she remembered Xerxes moving over her on the bed last night, his body so close to hers as he slowly undid her garters and pulled her silk stockings off her legs. She could still feel the intensity of his mouth on hers when he'd kissed her on the plane. She touched her lips as she recalled how his lips had seared her, how he'd crushed her to his chest and taken her in a hard, hungry embrace, his tongue sweeping her own as he—

"Good morning."

She looked up from the bed with a gasp, yanking her sheets back up to her neck.

Xerxes leaned in the doorway, dressed casually in khaki shorts and a black tank top that revealed his tanned, muscular arms.

"Good morning," she choked out in reply.

"I hope you slept well." He gave her a darkly sensual look. "I unlocked your door. I'm here now to give you what you need."

Had he somehow guessed what she'd just been thinking?

"What?" she said in a strangled voice.

He sat down on the bed beside her. "Here."

He placed a silver tray in her lap that held a silver coffeepot, chocolate croissants, fresh fruit, fried potatoes and orange juice. Staring down at it, her mouth watered. "You brought me breakfast?" she said numbly.

"You looked hungry last night."

She was. But something else caught her eye. Surprised, she reached across the tray to a bud vase that held a tiny pink rose. She breathed in the delicate scent of the bloom. "And this? Am I supposed to eat this?"

He shrugged. "It reminded me of you."

"*You* picked a flower?"

"I do know how," he said dryly. "I have my gardener grow them in our greenhouse in winter." He paused. "My grandmother grew polyantha rose bushes, fairy roses. They were the only bit of beauty we had then—her weeping rose tree." He looked at the tiny flower. "It's so delicate, the bloom's barely bigger than my thumb, and yet it's stronger than it looks. It resists disease, poor soil. Even men." He gave a slight smile. "The thorns are vicious."

She looked at the flower, then him, still shocked.

"It's my way of saying I'm sorry for the way I kidnapped you," he said with a sigh. "If I'd known you were innocent, that you hadn't deliberately set out to replace Laetitia, I would have…" Leaning back, he raked the back of his dark hair with his hand, then gave her a crooked grin. "Well, I would still have kidnapped you, but I'd have been more courteous about it."

"Oh," she said faintly. It made her nervous to have him so close to her again. He was freshly shaved and brutally handsome. And the smile he was giving her now was nothing short of devastating. Quickly, she looked back at the breakfast tray. "This looks delicious. I suppose now you'll tell me you cooked it yourself?"

"No." His sensual mouth quirked. "But I run a full-service prison here. Room and board included."

"Nice." She lifted her eyes to him suddenly. "It would be even nicer if you'd let me go."

He blinked, then his eyes hardened. "But we already agreed that I am not nice. I am a businessman. And you are too thin. No more diets. You will eat."

"I wasn't on a diet," she said, stung. "I wasn't even trying to lose weight. I just couldn't relax around Lars. I never had an appetite."

"You found him unappetizing? Shocking," Xerxes said, lifting his eyebrow. "But you are in my care now. Further starvation will cause you to lose your value. You will obey me in this."

Rose scowled at his tyrannical tone, then looked down at the tray. The coffee smelled divine, the croissants looked flaky and buttery. Her stomach grumbled. She hadn't eaten a thing since yesterday. Or was it the day before? She hadn't even eaten a slice of wedding cake. Cake with buttercream frosting was normally her favorite, but she hadn't been able to eat a bite.

Why hadn't she listened to what her body had been trying to tell her all along?

So rather than argue with him, she took a deep breath and placed the napkin in her lap. She took a bite of chocolate croissant, and her eyes widened. "Yum!" she breathed, and quickly ate another bite, and another.

"That's what I like," he said approvingly.

She took a big swig of orange juice. "I can relax around you, Xerxes. I don't need to be perfect for you—" she gave him a sudden grin "—because you're basically a terrible person."

"I am," he agreed. Leaning forward, he suddenly stroked her upper lip.

Electrified, she stared up at him in shock. "Why did you do that?"

"Orange juice on your lip," he said.

She swallowed. How could he do that? How could Xerxes, with just one touch, make her completely forget who she was and what she was doing?

"Go on," he said. "Don't stop now. I want you nice and healthy when I trade you."

Her smile faded.

Trade. Yes. Of course he wanted her healthy, so he could trade her like a horse. Fat and sassy, like a farm cow. Maybe he'd even find a way to sell her by the pound. Biting her lip, she looked down at her tray.

"How can you be so sure he'll still trade me?" she

said in a small voice. "Lars is married. He can't love me. If you're married, you can't love anyone else."

Xerxes's black eyes gleamed. "You really believe that."

"Of course I do!" she said fiercely, looking up. "He doesn't love me, and I don't...*can't*...love him ever again."

"Why not?" he said curiously. "Växborg is still a baron. Once he's divorced, he'll be free to legally wed you. But he will no longer have Laetitia's fortune. Is that the problem?"

She choked out a laugh. "I don't care about money. I've been broke for years. I know how to deal with it."

"So?"

"*He lied to me.* And it's more than that. Marriage is forever. Promises aren't just words. When I marry," she said, "it will be to a man who knows what a promise means."

His eyebrows lifted.

"You surprise me," he murmured. "I never expected any woman, let alone a woman who looks like you, to be..."

"To be what?" she demanded.

"Old-fashioned," he said quietly. "A woman who believes in honor and commitment? A woman who cannot be bought?" He shook his head. "I didn't know there were any such left in the world."

Rose's cheeks went hot. Was he mocking her, calling her a fool? She already felt like enough of one for a whole lifetime.

"It's not so rare," she said defensively, folding her

arms. "Lots of people feel that way in my hometown. Especially in my family," she muttered.

Her family. She bit her lip. What had Lars told them about her? Were they worried? Scared? Angry? She unfolded her arms and looked at him pleadingly. "Won't you let me call my mother and tell her what's happened?"

His eyebrows lowered as he shook his head. "Sorry. Too risky. Your mother might call the police. I know Lars will not."

"All right," she whispered, looking away. "I still don't understand how he could do such a horrible thing as pretend to marry me."

Xerxes cupped her chin, forcing her to meet his gaze. His black eyes went through her, causing a flicker of heat against her skin, spreading down her body. He moved closer to her, so close that she felt consumed by the black fire of his gaze. "He wanted to make sure no other man could have you."

No *other* man? Try *no man ever.* She took a deep breath. What would he say if he knew he was actually the first man who'd ever kissed her? Would he think she was a freakish old maid?

She covered her face with her hands. "I feel pathetic."

"Rose." Xerxes's voice was low. "I was wrong to call you naive. You...you just believe the best of people. It's a rare quality."

She felt the warmth of his arms start to encircle her. No! She couldn't let him touch her, or she might completely collapse back into his arms. She jerked back away from him on the bed, looking up at him fiercely.

"If you believe that, let me call my family and tell them I'm safe!"

He blinked. "I'm sure Lars told them that."

She thought of her parents, her grandparents, her brothers and sisters and nieces and nephews, and choked back her tears, causing her throat to throb. "No. I need to talk to them *now*."

"I already gave you my answer. No." He abruptly stood up from the bed. "There are a variety of new clothes in the closet for your stay. Enjoy your breakfast."

He left. Rose stared at the closed door.

With a weary sigh, she rose from the bed and went to the closet. There, just as he'd promised, she found an entirely new wardrobe, laundered and pressed, in a variety of sizes.

She ran her hands over all the hanging clothes softly, then looked at the shoes stacked neatly beneath.

There was every style of clothing possible, every-thing any woman could want—from bikinis and cocktail dresses to oversized sweatpants and T-shirts. Schlubby to chic and everything in between.

Very unlike Lars, who'd always had a very specific way he'd wished her to dress. He hadn't even allowed her to pick out her own wedding dress. *"You're beautiful in anything, petal,"* he'd said. *"But I prefer you to wear the jewels and furs you deserve."*

She'd tried to tell him that she didn't feel comfortable in those things, but he never listened to her. So she'd worn his fancy clothing in the hope it would make her feel like she belonged in his aristocratic set.

Grimly, she went back to the bed and poured herself some hot coffee into a pretty china teacup on the tray.

Taking a sip of the steaming black coffee, she stared at herself in the vanity mirror.

She looked awful. Like a raccoon with circles under her eyes, or maybe a Halloween ghost, pale and thin. Yesterday's wedding makeup was still smeared on her face, black mascara dark beneath her eyes from weeping.

With Lars constantly telling her she was perfect, when she knew she wasn't, she'd been afraid to stick up for herself or even, heaven forbid, start a fight. She'd told herself she was just inexperienced at dealing with relationships. Couples were supposed to compromise, weren't they?

But instead of compromise, she'd given herself up completely—when all he'd offered her in return were lies.

Rose choked down another sip of black coffee. Her eyes fell upon the wedding dress, still lying in a crumpled heap on the floor where Xerxes had dropped it the night before. Crossing the room in her bare feet, she picked up the couture gown with two fingers and dragged it into the trash.

There. It was gone. Brushing off her hands, she turned her back on it and felt immediately better. And then—*she was hungry.*

Going back to the breakfast tray, she dumped three heaping spoonfuls of sugar into her coffee, followed by copious amounts of real cream. She took a long drink of the hot, fragrant coffee and it was so sweet and creamy that she gasped with pleasure. She reached back for the buttery, freshly made chocolate croissant and polished it off in three bites.

Carrying the tray to the vanity table, she ate a big bite of sweet roll. Still chewing vigorously, she pulled Lars's expensively tarty lingerie off her body and dropped it onto the floor. She stared at it for a moment, then kicked it into the trash as well.

Going into the ensuite bathroom, she turned on the shower. Beneath the hot water, she scrubbed her face clean with a rough washcloth, washing off all the old smeared makeup from yesterday, rubbing at her skin until it was half-raw.

Toweling herself off afterward, she automatically looked around for a hair dryer. Then she stopped herself. No. No more hair dryer. No flatiron. No more fuss.

Going back into the bedroom, she flung open a drawer and found a wireless bra and comfortable white cotton panties that would actually cover her backside. Looking through the closet, she bypassed the fancy satin cocktail gowns and reached for a soft cotton skirt and a tissue-thin knit top. After getting dressed, she looked at herself again in the vanity mirror and took a deep breath.

She looked like her old self again. Regular old Rose Linden from California, the waitress who was working toward a college degree, the loving daughter who brought her parents homemade candy on weekends, who babysat for her nieces and nephews on Friday nights. No jewels, no furs, no tiara. *Just her.*

But her eyes had changed. They were exhausted and puffy from weeping, but it was more than that. Though still a virgin and no longer a bride, Rose knew she would never completely return to the idealistic girl she'd been.

But without all the makeup and confining clothes, letting her long blond hair air dry into its natural wave rather than wasting a precious hour of her life with the flatiron, she felt a new freedom. She went out to the chair and table by the window. Opening the screen door, she looked out at the view as she ate the rest of her breakfast, devouring the fresh fruit, potatoes and buttery pastries with equal relish.

She felt light. Freedom coursed in waves against her skin, as cool and refreshing as the soft sea breeze blowing through the window. Setting down her coffee cup beside her empty plate, she wandered outside on the balcony and looked out at the blue Aegean. The air was warm and smelled of salt and flowers and freshly exotic scents from faraway lands.

Last night, she'd been overwrought and exhausted and afraid. This villa had seemed full of darkness and shadows. But today, in the sunshine, she saw that it was beautiful. Bright pink flowers laced over white stucco on the edge of the bright blue sea.

As the cool morning wind blew against the bare skin of her legs and the tissue-thin cotton of her T-shirt, she closed her eyes in pleasure, turning her face toward the sun like a flower that had been deprived of it too long. For the first time in three months, she didn't feel jittery or stressed. She felt…happy.

"Buy it then." Xerxes's low voice floated up from below. "But not until the price hits forty. By then their shareholders will be screaming and they'll have no choice but to sell."

Looking down with an intake of breath, Rose saw

him pacing by the shaded grove near the pool as he spoke into his cell phone.

Khaki shorts revealed the strength of his thighs. The black tank top showed his broad shoulders and taut waistline as sunlight glistened off well-muscled arms.

He looked different to her today, too. The sunlight, now moving against the gray clouds, softened the hard lines of his face. He no longer seemed so fearsome and brutal. He just looked ruggedly handsome. And strong.

Was it because she no longer feared him? She no longer hated him, either. How could she? If Xerxes hadn't kidnapped her from the castle last night, she would have given herself to Lars in bed, believing she was his wife. She would have made the biggest mistake of her life.

All along, her body had told her something was wrong with Lars. The more often he'd insisted to Rose that she was absolutely perfect in every way, the more imperfect she'd felt. Rose knew she was a goofball, impulsive, and all kinds of other silly things, not perfect at all. Besides, what did love—real love, the kind that lasted a lifetime—have to do with sterile, frozen perfection?

All along, her body had known he was wrong for her. Her body—so much smarter than her brain!

"Fine." Still speaking into his phone, Xerxes suddenly lifted his head and looked right at her.

Sucking in her breath, she jumped back on the balcony, back into the shadows. A moment later, she heard his phone snap closed.

"Rose," he said with a low laugh. "I can see you."

She stepped forward, blushing with embarrassment.

"Oh, hello," she said, wincing at her own pathetic effort to sound casual. "I, er, didn't see you there."

Xerxes just gave her a lazy smile. "Just come down," he said. "I want to show you something."

"Oh, hello," she said, jerking at her wet pajama. Then in sound control. "I see, that's your phone—"

Xerxes had given her a long smile. "Look, angel," he'd said, "I want to show you something."

CHAPTER EIGHT

FROM the instant Rose had come out on the balcony, Xerxes had felt her presence like the first burst of sunlight at dawn.

He'd pretended not to see her at first. He'd continued to pace as he spoke, as was his habit when he was making deals over the phone that were worth hundreds of millions of dollars. But as he discussed business with his vice president of the Novros Group in New York, Xerxes had secretly watched Rose with hooded eyes.

Her expression was in shadow, but he could see her body. Long, wavy blond hair now hung damply down her shoulders, over a thin top that clung to her full breasts and tiny waist. A knee-length skirt revealed impossibly long legs, slender and strong.

Looking up at her, his whole body had tightened painfully. There was something about this girl—except *girl* wasn't the right word. Rose Linden was absolutely a woman. But there was something different about her, some quality of innocence that made her seem even younger than she was.

As he watched her, a strange need had trembled through his body that he'd never felt before. He did not like the feeling. He—Xerxes Novros—needed no one.

He barely knew her, and yet she had some power over him, a power his own body gave her. He understood, more and more, why Växborg had been willing to risk anything and defy anyone to possess her.

"Fine," he bit out, finishing the call. He looked back up at the balcony, deliberately allowing his eyes to meet hers. She instantly jumped back as if she'd been burned, shrinking back into the shadows of the balcony.

So she felt it then, too, this strange connection between them.

Xerxes still remembered the way she trembled when he'd kissed her on the plane. He'd called her *clumsy* and it had been true. For a beautiful woman, she'd been astonishingly inept. He still recalled the way her lips had moved so tremulously against his own, as if she had no idea how to move her lips into a kiss. But clumsy was only part of it. He hadn't told her the rest—that somehow, it had also been the most erotic kiss he'd ever experienced. He'd felt the passion of her brief surrender in a way that nearly brought him to his knees with the force of his own desire.

And then she'd slapped him.

He'd known from that moment that he would have her. Innocent or not, he would have her.

His promise not to kiss her until she begged for it was real, but it was strategic. He wouldn't break his word. He wouldn't have to. After that kiss, when he'd felt her passion and fire, he'd known it would be the easiest thing in the world to use her own sensuality against her and sweep her into bed.

In no time at all, she would beg him to kiss her. Just as every woman did.

Seducing Växborg's mistress before Xerxes traded her would be the final twist of the knife against his enemy. Especially since he would make sure Rose enjoyed it beyond measure.

Xerxes snapped his phone shut. He looked back at the empty balcony, covered by twisting bougainvillea in shadows as rapidly moving clouds passed over the morning sun.

"Rose," he said with a low laugh. "I can see you."

A moment later, she stepped forward, blushing. "Oh, hello," she said, visibly wincing. "I, er, didn't see you there."

Xerxes gave her a smile. "Come down," he said. "I want to show you something."

But she didn't immediately move to obey, as any other woman would have done. She just blinked at him, tilting her head. "What?"

Truthfully, he wanted to show her his bed, his naked body, and how thoroughly he could arouse her with his tongue, but all that would have to wait. "My house," he said smoothly. "You might be here for some time. You should know your way around."

"Thanks, but I'll just stay up here. In my room." *Where it's safe*, her tone seemed to imply.

He smiled up at her. "Come, Miss Linden. Your captivity doesn't have to be a prison. There's no reason you can't enjoy yourself while you're with me. Come downstairs."

She hesitated, then shook her head, her cheeks a charming shade of pink. "No, thanks, really. I'll, um, see you later," she said, then disappeared back into her bedroom.

She was afraid to even be around him. He almost laughed aloud. Seducing her would be even easier than he'd thought. If he were exceptionally clever he might have her flat on her back before noon.

If she wouldn't come downstairs, he would go to her. Whistling an old Greek folk song, Xerxes walked back inside his sprawling villa and went down the hallway toward the stairs. His cell phone vibrated and he answered, "Novros."

"Let me talk to Rose," Lars Växborg demanded.

At the sound of the man's peevish, aristocratic voice, Xerxes veered from the hallway and went into his private office. He went to the far window with its magnificent view of the sea, and replied coolly, "Has your divorce been finalized yet?"

"Practically. I'm in Las Vegas. I've signed the papers. With all your influence and mine, it's been expedited. It's as good as done. Let me talk to her."

"No." Initiating a divorce meant nothing, as they both knew perfectly well. Until the final ruling, it could be canceled at any time. Xerxes sat down in his chair. "You can speak to Rose when we make the trade."

"Damn you! Have you touched her? Tell me! Have you kissed her?"

"Yes," Xerxes said with dark pleasure.

"You bastard!" Växborg choked out. "What else have you—"

"Just one kiss," Xerxes said, then added ominously, "so far."

"You filthy brute, don't you touch her! She's mine!"

Xerxes gave a low, deliberate laugh. "Complete your

divorce. Return Laetitia to me as fast as you can. Before I forget my duties as host and entertain myself with your would-be bride. Before I enjoy Rose's body in my bed, over and over, until she forgets your name."

"Don't touch her, you bastard!" Växborg nearly shrieked. "Don't even think about—"

Xerxes hung up, still smiling to himself. Then he heard a noise and looked up.

Rose was standing in the open doorway, her mouth wide.

"You heard?" he said finally.

"I just came...came downstairs to see...to see..." She swallowed, staring across the shadowy office. Her beautiful face looked stricken as she whispered, "You intend to seduce me just to hurt Lars? Your promise not to kiss me was a lie?"

"No, Rose, listen—"

She put her hands over her ears. "Don't even try to explain. You're a liar," she said, backing away. "Just like *him*!"

Turning, she ran out of the office.

With a muttered curse Xerxes raced after her. She was astonishingly fast for a woman so petite, and ran all the way down the hall and out the back door of the villa before he was even out of his office. Outside, he pursued her past the pool and halfway up the hillside, toward the vineyard.

The sky had grown dark with gray clouds as he grabbed her. She struggled to escape, clawing at him, her chest lifting beneath her snug, thin top with every pant of her breath. "Let me go!"

He pushed her against a rough stone wall. "Quit

calling me a liar. I always keep my promises," he ground out. "Always."

"But you said—"

"I insinuated the worst to Växborg because I want him scared of what I might do to you. It is the only way he will divorce Laetitia and give up her fortune."

Rose abruptly stopped struggling. Tears were streaming down her eyes. "Why are you so determined to save her?" she whispered. "Who is she to you? Tell me!"

"Don't tell anyone. Ever." Xerxes remembered the fury in Laetitia's dark, beautiful eyes as they'd spoken for the first and last time. *"It wasn't enough for you to destroy my father. Now you want to kill my mother as well? You must never speak a word of this to anyone. Promise me."*

Now, in the distance, Xerxes heard thunder rolling low across the sky. He could still feel the same bleak hollowness in his gut he'd felt that day.

He looked down at Rose in his arms, so petite, so impossibly beautiful. He heard the whisper of her breath. He looked into her wide turquoise eyes, a sea of emotion for a man to drown in. Her pink, full mouth, natural and bare of makeup, parted as she licked her lips.

Clenching his hands into fists, he released her.

"I did not lie," he said in a low voice. "I will not kiss you unless you ask me."

Beneath the deepening shadows of the approaching storm, Rose looked up at him, tilting her head. "You don't intend to seduce me?"

"I want to seduce you," he said in a low voice. "It's all I can think about. But I gave you my word. I won't so much as kiss you."

She took a deep breath. "Oh." She stared down at the ground. "Lars said he still wanted to trade for me?"

"He arrogantly assumes he will win back your heart."

Clenching her jaw, she shook her head vehemently. "Never." She lifted her luminous eyes to his. "You know, you saved me from making the greatest mistake of my life yesterday. And you are keeping your promise to me. So you can't be all bad. I was thinking you can't be…"

"I am," he bit out. "All bad."

"But you're risking everything to save Laetitia," she said softly. "That is hardly selfish."

"I am saving her for my own reasons. Because…"

"Because?"

"Because I made a promise to protect her."

Rose gave a slow nod. "Which just proves my point."

Xerxes gave a low laugh. He took pride in keeping his word, starting with the promise he'd made to himself as a young, scared, lonely boy of five, abandoned by both parents, when he'd sworn he would someday find them again.

"I keep my promises," he said grimly. A flash of lightning illuminated the dark clouds. "That doesn't make me good."

"Who is Laetitia, Xerxes? Tell me." Rose moved closer, looking up into his face. A moment ago, she'd been angry, but now, she was touching his arm, her gaze curious and tender. "Is she your friend?"

Her small hand rested lightly on his skin, and he shuddered beneath that gentle touch. He had to fight the impulse to draw his arm away—or crush her small body beneath the force of his embrace. "It doesn't matter."

"Your...lover?"

He looked away.

"Do you love her?"

Xerxes turned to look down at her, his eyes locking with hers as the first drops of rain started to fall from the gray sky.

"Yes," he bit out. "I love her."

CHAPTER NINE

XERXES loved this other woman. His stark words caused a tremble through Rose's heart, a whisper of pain that she couldn't understand. She swallowed. "And you think once she's in your care, you can save her. You think you can wake her."

"Her marriage has doomed her to die," he said in a low voice. "I won't allow that to happen."

Rose looked at him, her heart in her throat. He loved a woman so much he was determined to save her at any cost to himself. That was true love, she thought. The kind that would sacrifice anything, do anything, for the beloved. "You really love her," she breathed, "don't you?"

"So?" he said coldly, then his black eyes widened. His lips twisted sardonically. "Ah. You are imagining I am some white knight in a fairy tale."

"Aren't you?"

He snorted scornfully. "You are quite the romantic, aren't you?"

He said the words like an insult. Rose blushed. "Just because I can see the best of people, then—"

"You are wrong about me." Xerxes's eyes glittered.

"And you're wrong to have such blind faith. Your noble-hearted knight does not exist."

Rose took a deep breath. "I believe he does. I'll wait. I'll have faith."

He laughed, a hard, ugly sound. "Faith is a lie that fools tell themselves in the night."

She stared at him. "Do you really believe that?"

Xerxes turned out to face the sea.

She looked at the taut lines of his body. The tanned, muscular arms. Her eyes traced the dark shadow of his jaw, the mussed wave of his black hair.

Her arms started to reach out to comfort him before she caught herself. Why would her body reach to comfort him? She always worried about other people's feelings but she was way off here, being concerned about him. Xerxes Novros was powerful and rich. He could get any woman he wanted—and probably did. So why would Rose possibly think she could comfort him? Or even that he needed comfort?

Faith is a lie that fools tell themselves in the night. It was the most heartbreaking thing she'd ever heard.

"Maybe you're right," she said slowly. She shook her head. "But a life without faith, without being brave enough to risk loving someone and be loved in return, is no life at all."

His jaw tightened. "I measure success differently. On how I keep my word."

It was almost unbearable now for Rose to keep still, to resist the urge to wrap her arms around him and ask what had left such a deep scar on his heart. Rose had to force her arms to remain at her sides, her hands tightening into fists with the effort it took not to reach her arms around him.

"But such honor is meaningless without love," she said in a low voice. "And you must know that already. It's why you're desperate to save Laetitia. Because you love her."

Slowly, he turned toward her. "It's not what you think."

"It's not?"

He didn't answer. She took a deep breath and changed the subject. "But what if your plan doesn't work?" she said in a small voice. "What if Lars won't trade her for me after all?"

"It has to work." He blinked, his eyes briefly bleak. "It must."

Rose's heart felt anguished in sympathy for the dark, powerful man before her, who looked so haunted and alone. But just as she could bear it no longer and started to reach for him, Xerxes's eyes widened to stare at a point behind her ear. He called out in Greek, and she whirled around to see a bodyguard approaching them rapidly, hurrying up the hillside. The hulking man spoke into Xerxes's ear.

Xerxes's eyes went wide. He inhaled a deep breath that expanded his chest, then turned to her. "Time to go."

"Go?" she stammered. "Where?"

"Right now."

"Why?" she said, bewildered.

Xerxes seems strangely back to his old self as he grinned. "I have a new desire to see a tropical beach."

She looked out in shock and pointed towards the sea. "What do you call that?"

"Rainy and cold."

"It's warm!"

"But not hot." He put his hand on her shoulder and looked down into her eyes with a deep, smoldering heat. "And I want to see you in a bikini."

"Where?"

But Xerxes just turned and headed for the villa with the bodyguard. She stared at him in shock. What had changed his mood?

Rose stomped her foot in confusion, then yelled after him, far too late, "Wherever we're going, if you think I'm going to wear a bikini for you, you're crazy!"

By late afternoon, they had arrived via private jet to an island in the crystal blue waters of the Indian Ocean. Above a white, sandy beach, palm trees swayed in the hot breeze.

"Where are we?" Rose stammered, yawning from her nap as they climbed out of the SUV.

"The Maldives," he said simply. She turned to stare at him in shock.

"How many islands do you own anyway?" she said faintly.

He gave a hearty laugh. "I don't own this one. We're at a resort owned by a friend of mine, Nikos Stavrakis. He's assigned a full-time housekeeper to this cottage exclusively for our stay. The bodyguards will be at the gatehouse a mile down the road."

Taking her hand, Xerxes escorted her into a small yellow cottage on a private, secluded beach. Inside the main living area, a fan moved the air from the high wooden ceiling. Through the wall of windows, she saw a private pool and veranda beside the white beach and azure waters, beneath swaying palm trees.

Rose had read about Stavrakis resorts. They were swanky hotels for rich people, the kind of glamorous places she read about in celebrity gossip magazines. Utterly out of reach of a regular person like her.

She glanced around the cottage. Cozy as it was, on a private beach with devoted housekeeper, she still wouldn't be surprised if it cost ten thousand dollars a night.

And they would be sharing this intimate space alone. She looked back at Xerxes, and the cottage suddenly seemed a little smaller.

"There's no television," he said. "But I don't think you'll miss it."

She licked her lips. "Why not? What will we be doing?"

"A selection of new books and magazines has been provided for you. The housekeeper will prepare delicious meals and clean and do anything else you need. You'll have nothing to do but sit on the beach and work on your tan."

She stared at him. Then she scowled. "Meaning—I can't leave."

"You have no need to."

But it meant she couldn't sneak into the local village to look for an Internet café or try to telephone her family. She looked around her. There wasn't even a phone here, much less a computer with a modem.

"Do you like the cottage?"

She glared at him. "Sure. It's lovely—for a prison."

"If you wish to regard it that way."

"How else should I see it?"

"You could call it a vacation." Lifting a dark eyebrow, he gave her a wicked half smile. His eyes traced her body. "It's a pity we had no time to pack in Greece. Fortunately I've arranged a new wardrobe for you here."

He pushed open the sliding doors to reveal the bedroom. Walking to a closet, he opened the doors.

Peering past him, Rose saw an arrangement of bikinis and several little beach cover-ups, scandalizingly short robes of thin cotton lace or translucent gauze. That was it. There was nothing else to wear. Her eyes widened. Leaning back, she put her hands on her hips and scowled at him. "Where's the rest?"

"Oh. Is there nothing in there but bikinis for you?" he said innocently.

But it was worse than that. She sucked in her breath as, looking further inside the closet, she saw men's T-shirts and shorts. A sinking feeling went through her heart. "Why are your clothes in my closet?"

He came behind her, not touching, but close enough that she could feel the warmth from his body. "This is a honeymoon cottage. There is only one bedroom. And only one bed."

The honeymoon cottage.

"Oh," she managed to say with suddenly dry lips. She jerked away, choking out, "I'll take the couch, then."

He looked down at her. "You will take the bed."

"That wouldn't be fair." Even as she told herself that he was her captor and deserved to suffer, she felt guilty about kicking him to the couch. He'd promised he wouldn't touch her and she was starting to believe him. Hesitantly, she said, "I suppose we could share...."

"No," he cut her off roughly.

"Why?"

"Being close to you when I am forbidden to touch you... There's only so much a man can take. Unless you actually *want* to make me suffer?"

Their eyes locked, and for an instant, she forgot to breathe. Then she blinked. "A little suffering on your part might be nice, yes," she said with an impish smile.

His returning smile rose slowly across his face, and without realizing what she was doing, she leaned forward on her toes.

"Sir." A bodyguard entered the front room with a loud rap at the door, and they both whirled toward him. Exhaling, Xerxes gave him a quick nod. "Excuse me," he said, turning back to her. "I must leave you now."

"But we just got here!"

"I have something urgent to do. I will return later." He stroked her cheek. "I've arranged for the housekeeper to serve dinner on the beach."

Squeezing her hand, he left. Rose stared after him in shock.

After he left, she walked along the beach and explored the lush grounds behind the cottage. It was strange to be so alone in this beautiful place. Crossing through a tropical garden, she stopped as her jaw dropped when she saw two large weeping rose trees.

Pink fairy roses. Xerxes's favorite flower. Growing

wild on this island in the Indian Ocean, thousands of miles from Greece.

Resolutely, she turned and walked away. Then, after five steps, she stopped. Whirling, she went back to the nearest rose tree. Careful not to pierce her fingertips with thorns, she picked one of the tiny pink blooms. Returning to the cottage, she carefully put it in water in a tiny bud vase she found in the stocked modern kitchen.

Hours of sunshine later, she finally put aside the novel she was reading on the lanai in the deepening afternoon. She'd been alone all day long at a luxury beach house. She'd had a lovely lunch served to her by the housekeeper. Reading a fabulous novel and watching the sunlight sparkle across the blue waters of the Indian Ocean, kidnapped or not, she should have been having a decent time.

But she wasn't. She was missing something. Or *someone*.

The thought brought her up short. She couldn't miss Xerxes's company. Ridiculous. He was her captor! If she occasionally found him amusing or entrancing she was merely making the best of a bad situation, that was all.

But they'd spent the long flight here talking. He'd sat right beside her, plying her with Greek dishes, asking her interested, sympathetic questions about her family and home.

She'd answered in monosyllables at first, giving him one tart reply after another. But instead of being offended, he'd seemed to enjoy the repartee. And his undivided attention had been strangely...*pleasurable*.

She'd felt his arm along the back of the white leather sofa behind her, so close to her body, and she'd trembled. Every time he looked at her, the intensity and heat of his dark gaze turned her inside out.

Rose didn't want to think about it now. Or why she'd not only noticed his favorite flower in a lush garden, but she'd also picked a rose for him and placed it in water.

Looking up from her book, she noticed the dark-haired, plump young housekeeper struggling to carry a table across the beach to a spot overlooking the surf. Relieved to leave the lanai and lounge chair and all her disconcerting thoughts behind her, Rose got to her feet and hurried down to the beach. "Wait! Can I help?"

The housekeeper, who looked only a few years older than Rose, shook her head, even though she looked as if she were fighting back tears.

"Really?" Rose bit her lip. "Please, Mrs. Vadi, won't you let me help?"

"No," the woman said, then burst into tears. Within minutes, Rose had learned the woman was grieving for her husband, who'd died six months before, and that she was worried about her feverish eight-year-old daughter, whom she'd had to leave at home alone.

"But I can't lose this job, miss," the woman gasped, wiping her eyes fiercely. "If I do, I won't be able to keep a roof over my child's head."

"Go home!" Rose said, sympathetic tears welling in her own eyes.

"I can't."

"Mr. Novros will never know you're gone." When the woman still hesitated, Rose grabbed her sleeve. "Please, it's such a small thing," she whispered. "I'm so far away from my own family. Let me at least help yours."

The housekeeper wept and embraced her, then gave her detailed instructions about how to make the dinner, instructions Rose found herself unable to remember when she faced the stainless-steel kitchen alone half an hour later. After several inedible attempts, she gave up and prepared her own favorite dinner instead. As the rice noodles bubbled, Rose went outside and finished setting up the table by the beach.

She cast an anxious look at the sun lowering in the west in streaks of red and orange. Expecting Xerxes to return any moment, she hurried to the cottage, where she showered and brushed her hair. What to wear? Beachwear was all she had, thanks to him. Scowling, she went back to the wardrobe. She briefly considered wearing one of Xerxes's T-shirts or khaki shorts, but the thought of wearing his clothing was too intimate. That would be the action of a lover, which—she told herself firmly—she would never be.

Ultimately, she wore two gauzy beach cover-ups layered over a pale pink bikini. She surveyed her modest look with satisfaction. The two robes together blocked her body from view. She smiled at herself in the mirror, anticipating his reaction. That would teach him!

Carrying out the dinner tray, she impulsively grabbed the pink rose she'd picked in the garden, still in a bud vase, and placed it in the center of the table. Then she sat down and waited, staring across the white sand beach toward the red and purple sunset streaking the sparkling sapphire ocean.

She jerked awake as she felt Xerxes shaking her

shoulder. With a start, Rose realized she'd fallen asleep with her head cradled in her arms on the table.

It was now almost dark. His silhouette was black against the fading red sunset. He'd changed on the plane, but she saw that his jeans and T-shirt were dusty, and his face was grim. His good mood of just a few hours before had evaporated.

"What's wrong?" she said. "What's happened?"

"Forget it," he said heavily, sitting in the chair next to her.

"Where have you been?"

He shook his head bitterly. "It doesn't matter." He looked at the flower. "Where did that rose come from?"

She bit her lip. Had she done something wrong, something that would reveal that she'd sent the housekeeper home? "Why do you ask?" she evaded.

"The rose," he said, then looked up at her. "I heard it was the national flower of these islands, but I've never been to this resort. I'm not known by the staff. Is it a coincidence? Or did you request it for me?"

"It was nothing, really," she said awkwardly. Her cheeks felt burning hot. "I found them in the garden. I was surprised to see the same roses here, growing thousands of miles from your home. I thought you'd like it. That's all."

"I do," he said quietly. "Thank you."

Taking the rose out of the vase, he reached across the table and tucked it behind her ear, in her long, wavy blond hair. His hand trailed slowly down from her ear, caressing her cheek. Then he took her hand in his own, across the table, and she shivered in the warm night.

Overhead, the sky was streaked with red and purple like the echoes of ash and fire. Like the fire slowly smoldering in his dark eyes as he looked at her. Like the fire that was filling her body with the bewildering ache of desire.

"I'm sorry I'm so late," he murmured, then looked at the covered silver dish. "Dinner must be long cold." He sighed with regret. "I've been dreaming for the last hour about the dinner the housekeeper would prepare for us. Maldivian food is supposed to be spectacular, a mix of Indian, Asian and Middle Eastern flavors. Nikos has raved about her cooking more than once. I can hardly wait—"

With a flourish, he pulled the lid off the silver tray. And stared. He sat back into his chair with an amazed thump.

"Spaghetti bolognese?" he said faintly.

"Spaghetti is delicious," she said defensively.

He looked at her.

"And with rice noodles, too!" she said, taking the spoon from him. "That's certainly exotic! Shall I serve?"

Rose dumped some spaghetti on each plate, then looked down at her cold, rather unappetizing concoction. She'd had to improvise for ingredients. She'd used rice noodles for pasta, and since she hadn't found a handy can of marinara sauce or even tomato paste, she'd improvised by smashing fresh tomatoes into a rudimentary sauce. She'd added a mishmash of chopped mystery meat she'd found in the fridge with whatever spices she could find in the kitchen, and hoped for the best.

All right, so she wasn't always the best cook—except

where candy was concerned—but even she couldn't ruin something as simple as spaghetti, she hoped.

She took a bite, and discovered she was wrong.

It was *awful*. And cold, in the bargain. She nearly choked it out, then covered up her gag reflex with a cough before she managed to swallow it down. "Wow," she managed to say.

Xerxes took a bite and blanched. Standing up, he threw the napkin back on the table. "I don't know if the housekeeper was drunk in the kitchen, or if this is a joke, but I'm going to register a complaint—"

"No!" Rose grabbed his wrist, looking up at him pleadingly. "It's not her fault. It's mine!"

He looked down at her with a frown. "What?"

"I sent Mrs. Vadi home. I told her I'd make dinner and you wouldn't know the difference." Rose shook her head tearfully. "Don't tell her manager she left. If they knew, they might fire her and it's not her fault I botched dinner so badly!"

He slowly sat down, staring at her. "You sent her home? Why?"

"We got to talking and…her husband died recently and her little girl was sick at home alone. She needed help," she said, "so I helped her."

He gaped at her. "You—*got to talking*?" he said faintly. "I have employees who've worked for me for ten years and I don't know anything about their personal lives."

"That's too bad."

"I like it that way." He blinked, still looking bewildered. "But why you would volunteer to do her work, when you could have just relaxed on the beach? It's her job. Her responsibility. Not yours."

Rose looked out into the growing shadows of night, listening to the roar of the ocean waves. "I had to help her be with her little girl," she whispered, lifting her chin to meet his eyes. "Because all I want to do is talk to my own mother."

Silence fell between them.

"I can't risk it," he said quietly. "If you talk to your mother, she might contact U.S. authorities. A kidnapped young bride is just the sort of sensational story that would be splashed all over the international news."

"What if I gave you my word she wouldn't tell?" she said desperately.

He shook his head. "I'm sorry."

She stared down at her plate. "Anyway, I had to let Mrs. Vadi go home and be with her family tonight. Because I can't."

"I still don't understand."

"Don't you have a family?"

He blinked. "Not the way you mean."

"No siblings?"

"I was raised an only child."

"Your mother?"

"Dead."

"Your father?"

"No."

"That's dreadful," Rose said softly, her heart breaking. Looking at his profile in the darkening twilight, she tightened her fingers over his. "I'm so sorry."

For a moment, he didn't move. Then he pulled his hand away. "Let me guess," he said sardonically. "You lived in a big old house, your mother baked cookies when you came home from school and your father taught you how to ride your bike."

"Yes," she said simply.

"Of course." He looked away. "You had the fairy tale."

She stared at him. The fairy tale?

Standing up abruptly, he reached for her hands and pulled her to her feet. "Come on," he said gruffly. "This time, I'll make dinner."

The full moon had risen low over the horizon as they walked along the deserted beach to the honeymoon cottage. Pulling her into the modern kitchen, he turned on a light.

"I can help," she offered weakly.

"Absolutely not." He used the chopping knife in his hand to point at the kitchen table. "Sit there."

As she watched, he swiftly made two large turkey sandwiches, served with slices of ripe mango. He set both plates down on the kitchen table and sat beside her.

He popped open a small bottle of Indian beer and handed it to her, then clinked his bottle against hers with a grin. *"Bon appétit."*

The sandwich and fruit were delicious. As she ate, Rose looked at him in the sleek, dimly lit kitchen. His words still echoed through her mind.

You had the fairy tale.

She'd once thought marrying a handsome baron in a castle was the amazing dream. The truth was that she'd had the fairy tale all along.

She'd had family and friends she loved. She had a

small apartment of her own, with her childhood home just an hour away. She'd had enough money to pay her bills. So what if she'd had to hold down more than one job to make ends meet? So what if her car didn't always work well, or she had to jump-start it half the time to get to her night classes? She'd had a happy childhood. She'd had a happy life.

She'd been lucky beyond words.

"You're right," she said over the lump in her throat. "With my family, I mean. I guess I did have the fairy tale."

Finishing his sandwich, Xerxes took a sip of beer and looked at her. "You'll have it again." Moonlight from the window frosted his body, making him appear otherworldly, like a dark angel, as he leaned toward her. "A woman like you was born to have a happy life."

Her breathing quickened as his gaze fell to her mouth. He was going to kiss her. She could feel it. He stroked her cheek, tilting her head up toward his, and she could barely hear the roar of the ocean over the rapid beat of her heart.

"I've never met a woman like you before," he said softly, his black eyes searching hers as he stroked her bare forearm lightly with his fingertips. "You...amaze me."

This honeymoon cottage, so remote in the middle of a wide, distant ocean, seemed like their own distant world. His handsome, rugged face, the powerful curve of his body as he leaned toward her, the light feeling of his touch against her skin, made her brain stop working. She trembled, licking her lips. Would she fall into his arms when he kissed her? *Would she fall into his bed?*

He glanced down at her half-empty plate. "Are you finished?"

She stared up at him, unable to even say yes.

He smiled, then took her hand in his own. "Come."

He led her from the kitchen to the large sitting room and sat her down gently on the couch. Going back to the kitchen, he returned with a tray. She watched as he dropped fresh raspberries into a crystal flute. Popping open a bottle of expensive champagne, he poured it over the raspberries then held out the flute to her, watching her with his inscrutable dark eyes.

"What is this?" she whispered.

"I'm making it up to you."

"What?"

"I ruined your wedding night." When she didn't take the flute, he pressed it into her hand, wrapping his fingers around hers. She could barely breathe as she looked up at him, feeling his large hand wrapped around her smaller one. He said in a low voice, "I am going to make it up to you tonight."

"How?" she stammered.

He stepped back, his gaze still intensely upon her. She felt butterflies in her stomach and nervously drank the rest of the delicious raspberry-infused champagne. But the butterflies only increased. Xerxes silently refilled her champagne with a sensual promise in his dark gaze.

Then he left her, going into the adjacent white marble bathroom, with its bathtub built for two that overlooked the moonlit sea. He turned on the faucet, starting a hot, steamy bath, filling it with fragrant bubble bath.

FREE Merchandise is 'in the Cards' for you!

Dear Reader,

We're giving away FREE MERCHANDISE!

Seriously, we'd like to reward you for reading this novel by giving you **FREE MERCHANDISE** worth over **$20**. And no purchase is necessary!

You see the Jack of Hearts sticker above? Paste that sticker in the box on the Free Merchandise Voucher inside. Return the Voucher promptly...and we'll send you valuable Free Merchandise!

Thanks again for reading one of our novels—and enjoy your Free Merchandise with our compliments!

Pam Powers

Pam Powers

P.S. Look inside to see what Free Merchandise is **"in the cards"** for you!

W

e'd like to send you two free books to introduce you to the Harlequin Presents° series. These books are worth over $10, but they are yours to keep absolutely FREE! We'll even send you 2 wonderful surprise gifts. You can't lose!

YOUR FREE MERCHANDISE INCLUDES...

2 FREE Harlequin Presents® Books

AND 2 FREE Mystery Gifts

FREE MERCHANDISE VOUCHER

2 FREE BOOKS
and
2 FREE GIFTS

Please send my Free Merchandise, consisting of
2 Free Books and **2 Free Mystery Gifts**.
I understand that I am under no obligation to buy
anything, as explained on the back of this card.

*About how many NEW paperback fiction books
have you purchased in the past 3 months?*

☐ 0-2   ☐ 3-6   ☐ 7 or more
E9HY   **E9JC**   **E9JN**

☐ I prefer the regular-print edition   ☐ I prefer the larger-print edition
106/306 HDL   **176/376 HDL**

Please Print

FIRST NAME

LAST NAME

ADDRESS

APT.#   CITY

STATE/PROV.   ZIP/POSTAL CODE

Offer limited to one per household and not applicable to series that subscriber is currently receiving.
Your Privacy—The Reader Service is committed to protecting your privacy. Our Privacy Policy is available online
at www.ReaderService.com or upon request from the Reader Service. We make a portion of our mailing list available
to reputable third parties that offer products we believe may interest you. If you prefer that we not exchange your
name with third parties, or if you wish to clarify or modify your communication preferences, please visit us at
www.ReaderService.com/consumerschoice.

NO PURCHASE NECESSARY!

The Reader Service - Here's how it works:

Accepting your 2 free books and 2 free mystery gifts (gifts valued at approximately $10.00) places you under no obligation to buy anything. You may keep the books and gifts and return the shipping statement marked "cancel." If you do not cancel, about a month later we'll send you 6 additional books and bill you just $4.05 each for the regular-print edition or $4.55 each for the larger-print edition in the U.S. or $4.74 each each for the regular-print edition or $5.24 each for the larger-print edition in Canada. That's a savings of at least 13% off the cover price. It's quite a bargain! Shipping and handling is just 50¢ per book.* You may cancel at any time, but if you choose to continue, every month we'll send you 6 more books, which you may either purchase at the discount price or return to us and cancel your subscription.

*Terms and prices subject to change without notice. Prices do not include applicable taxes. Sales tax applicable in N.Y. Canadian residents will be charged applicable taxes. Offer not valid in Quebec. All orders subject to approval. Books received may not be as shown. Credit or debit balances in a customer's account(s) may be offset by any other outstanding balance owed by or to the customer. Please allow 4 to 6 weeks for delivery. Offer available while quantities last.

"It's ready," he whispered, pulling her to her feet. She gripped his hand, feeling a little unsteady.

He pulled her into the elegant bathroom. Still holding her champagne flute, which had somehow been refilled again, she looked down at the enormous bathtub full of bubbles. Beyond it, an enormous open window overlooked the moonlit Indian Ocean. She felt the warm breeze off the lanai. Warm steam and the scent of exotic, spiced flowers filled the room.

She felt his touch move like silk against her waist as he opened the belts that held the two gauzy robes to her body. He dropped first one robe, then the other, to the marble floor.

Xerxes towered over Rose as he looked down at her, his eyes slowly tracing her body as she stood nearly naked in her pale pink bikini. He gave her a dark, sensual smile and a flash of heat raced over her body, causing a bead of sweat to break out between her breasts. What was his electricity that made her so weak, that left her shaking from the inside out?

The smile dropped from his sensual mouth.

"Take off your bikini," he whispered.

Without thinking, she reached up for the tie behind her neck. Then she realized what she was doing. She dropped her hand.

"I can't," she stammered. "Not with you right here."

"I'll turn around."

She had a sudden view of his broad-shouldered back in the form-fitting T-shirt as he turned around. She stared at his form, his slim hips in his jeans, the hard-muscled curve of his backside.

"Done?" he said without turning around.

With a jolt, she put her hands unsteadily to her head. Had she been *ogling* him? The bubbles of the champagne made her feel so strangely unlike herself.

But it wasn't just the champagne. She looked back at the fragrant, steaming bubble bath. She knew she should leave this room at once. She should tell Xerxes she had no interest in champagne or warmth or bubbles. She should go back into the bedroom alone and close the door. That was the sensible thing to do.

But she suddenly didn't want to be sensible.

She'd spent twenty-nine years waiting for her prince to come, saving herself for a man she could love forever. But what if he wasn't coming? What if, as Xerxes had said, her knight in shining armor did not even exist? What if she'd wasted all her youth yearning for a romantic dream that would never happen?

She was tired of being the girl who was always alone. Always waiting, as locked away from pleasure as any sleeping princess in a glass coffin.

Rose took a haggard breath. If she could not have the romantic dream everyone else in her family had, she would take what joy she could in the life that was left to her. She would take risks. She would be bold.

Slowly, Rose untied her bikini top and dropped it to the floor. She untied the bottom and kicked it away. Climbing naked into the bathtub, she sank beneath the fragrant white bubbles. Closing her eyes, holding her breath, she slid all the way down beneath the water.

When she rose up from the bath a moment later, her hair soaking wet, she felt reborn.

She heard a choked gasp behind her.

Xerxes was now standing by the bathtub, staring down at her. Following his eyes, she saw rivulets of water running between her breasts, saw her nipples flushed deep pink. They pebbled beneath his gaze.

With a gasp, she sank into the water, covering her body with thick white bubbles.

"You said you would turn around!" she said.

He gave a low laugh. "I never said I wouldn't turn back." He sat on the edge of the large tub and looked down at her. "You are so beautiful," he whispered, running his hand along her naked shoulder, visible above the bubbles. "The most magnificent woman I've ever seen."

She blushed. "You're just tipsy on champagne."

"I haven't had any champagne."

She blinked, glancing at the nearly empty bottle next to the bathtub. Who'd drunk all that, then? By the way her body felt pleasantly separated from her brain, the answer was appallingly clear. She shook her head. "You...are you trying to..."

"To what?"

"Get me drunk?" she blurted out.

His sensual mouth curved. "Why would I do that?"

"I don't know," she said. "You tell me."

He stroked her water-slicked blond hair curling over her collarbone. She looked up at him breathlessly, her neck tilting back. He leaned over her, his lips inches from hers. Her mouth inched toward his, wanting him to kiss her. *Willing* him to kiss her.

"Turn around," he ordered, and without thought she obeyed, turning her face toward the window.

She felt his hands fall heavily on her naked shoulders.

He began to slowly rub circles into the overwrought muscles of her neck and shoulders. She closed her eyes. It was bliss. It was heaven. It was...

Dangerous.

"So you think I am going to all this effort to seduce you," he said quietly.

Hearing him actually speak the words made her fears seem ludicrous. He was a powerful, ruthless millionaire with the world at his fingertips. And he'd told her he loved another woman—someone he intended to trade for Rose. She was just his captive, his pawn. Why would he go to such effort to seduce Rose, the ex-girlfriend of his enemy, a waitress and twenty-nine-year-old nobody? Her cheeks became hot. "I know that sounds ridiculous."

"You're right," he said quietly. "I am going to seduce you."

Her eyes flew open. As he continued to sensually rub her neck and shoulders, she stared wide-eyed out the window. In the silence, she saw the slender black silhouettes of palm trees swaying in front of the brilliant white clouds lit up by the moon, saw the stars twinkling in the night.

She felt the intense pleasure of his touch. Felt his strength. Felt his power.

When he leaned over her, she felt his breath against the crook of her neck, then his lips brushed the tender flesh of her earlobe.

"I want you." The whisper of his lips against her skin caused a sizzle of fire down her body. "And I intend to do everything I can to win you."

She felt dizzy, the world trembling all around her. She was naked in the warmth of the bath he'd drawn for her, tipsy on his expensive champagne. But most intoxicating of all was this feeling building inside her, this strange ache of forbidden desire. She felt his cotton shirt brush against her hair, felt the warmth of his muscular arms lean against hers.

She closed her eyes, waiting for him to seize her, turn her around in his arms and pull her into his hot embrace. Waiting for him to end this sweet torment.

He was going to kiss her...wasn't he?

"I want you, Rose," he whispered. "So much." He took a sudden deep, ragged breath, then said in a low voice, "But you deserve better than a man like me."

And suddenly, his warmth was gone.

Startled, she whirled around. In her movement, she splashed bathwater and bubbles wildly to the floor.

All she saw was his retreating back as he left her. Without a backward glance.

CHAPTER TEN

You deserve better than a man like me.

The next morning, Xerxes woke up stiff and sore from sleeping alone outside in the hammock on the beach. He still couldn't believe it.

He'd had her. Naked and ripe for the taking. He'd seen it in her body's reaction to his touch, in the quiver of her neck and shoulders beneath the stroke of his fingers, in the flush of heat on her skin.

He'd had her. Getting her to release him from his promise, luring her into just gasping out the words *kiss me* would have been the easiest thing in the world.

It had taken slightly longer than he'd thought it would, but he'd finally succeeded in getting her where he wanted her. Bedding Rose last night would have been at once his revenge—and his reward.

And yet he'd let her go. He'd stumbled away from the bathtub, and her body covered with bubbles, without a word. Once outside, he'd stripped off his dusty clothes and dived naked into the sea to clear his body of dust. To clear his soul of desire.

You deserve better than a man like me.

Now, raking his hand through his hair, he twisted his aching neck to crack the aching vertebrae. After sleeping outside all night, he cursed himself silently. Why had he let her go last night? Why had he shown such foolish *mercy?*

"I'll have faith…" He heard her voice like music, and remembered the way she'd looked at him with eyes of endless blue. *"A life without faith, without being brave enough to risk loving someone and be loved in return, is no life at all."*

Xerxes's lip curled. His frustration and lack of sleep were clearly melting his brain!

He'd come to the Maldives yesterday filled with optimism, after his chief bodyguard had told him Laetitia had been sighted here. He'd known if he could find her on his own and get her safely to good medical care, he would have no need to deal with Växborg. Once Laetitia was well, she could divorce him herself. And Xerxes—he could keep Rose for himself.

But after almost a year of repeated sightings that proved false, Xerxes should have known better than to hope. The small hut at the end of the dusty road on the other side of the island had been deserted. Talking to the neighbors, they discovered that someone who looked like Laetitia had indeed been there. But she'd been moved just two days before, and they did not know where she'd gone. Her caretaker, a toothless old woman who spoke no English and had no medical training, had been paid in cash. The woman said that the young sleeping woman still lived. That was all she knew.

Returning alone to the honeymoon cottage, Xerxes had been furious and angry—at Växborg, but even more at himself.

Why couldn't he find Laetitia?

Why couldn't he save her?

Why did he keep failing?

When Xerxes had seen Rose sleeping peacefully at the table on the beach, he'd stopped on the sand. She was alone beneath the sunset, ethereally sexy in those little gauzy robes over a bikini. And he'd suddenly known how he would take out his frustration. How he would take both his solace—and his pleasure.

Before he'd reached out his hand to shake her awake, he'd already decided that he would possess her. He wouldn't force her. He just wouldn't leave her any other choice.

No woman could resist a seduction as gentle as a question. Once secure in the false belief that she held all the power, a woman always surrendered. Power was a heady aphrodisiac.

And last night, Rose would have surrendered as well. *If he hadn't let her go.*

Why? He rubbed his forehead wearily. Why had he done it? Because he liked her? Because she had a good heart? Because he *admired* her?

He thought again of her beauty. Of her luscious body. And his eyes narrowed.

Next time, he would be ruthless.

"Did you really sleep out here all night?"

At the sound of her shy voice, he looked up to discover Rose standing awkwardly beside the hammock. She was wearing a little white cover-up of eyelet cotton and flip-flop sandals. Her face was bare and lightly tanned, her blond hair wavy and tumbling down her shoulders. She looked very young.

"Yes," he said shortly.

"You didn't have to do that, you know. You could have slept on the couch." She gave him a tremulous smile. "I don't bite."

"Maybe I do."

"I'm not afraid of you."

At her shining smile, an ache filled his chest that felt like pain.

Morning had dawned over the beach, streaking pink across the sky over the crystalline waves. A fresh breeze blew through the palm trees overhead, causing tendrils of her blond hair to curl across her beautiful face.

And it was then that he saw it in her face, bright as day. *Rose actually cared about him.*

The realization jolted him like a kick in the gut. He climbed out of the hammock so quickly that he nearly fell.

"Are you all right?"

"Fine." He straightened, irritated.

"Why did you leave like that last night?" she persisted, in spite of the clear signals. He didn't wish to discuss it.

"For your own good," he muttered.

"What?"

Angrily, he whirled on her. "Just leave it alone. Trust me. You slept better last night without my company."

She stared at him.

"No," she said in a low voice. "You're wrong. I didn't sleep at all." Her beautiful face was heartbreakingly angelic as she whispered, "I couldn't stop thinking about you."

Their eyes met, and he couldn't look away.

He wanted her so badly that his whole body thrummed with it. Painfully. Single-mindedly.

He wanted to take her right here on the deserted beach, to rip off her white cover-up in the pale pink morning, to push her naked body against the sand and kiss and suckle and taste every inch of her skin. He wanted to push himself inside her, to fill her completely, to ride her until she forgot every other lover, until she screamed his name.

Standing before her in yesterday's T-shirt and jeans, Xerxes held himself still. His hands clenched with the effort it took not to kiss her. "Why were you thinking about me?"

"You try to pretend you're selfish and cruel," she said softly. "But I keep thinking about you and coming to one conclusion. You're a good man."

He gave a low laugh, like thunder reverberating across the dark sky. "I am not good." Something snapped inside him and he reached for her shoulders, looking down into her eyes searchingly as he whispered, "But you...you are."

"Oh." She blushed. "I'm not so very good. I've been feeling quite stupid, actually, driving you away from your bed. The couch, I mean."

She was stammering, embarrassed. As if she had anything to feel guilty about, when it had been Xerxes who deliberately rented the honeymoon cottage to set the stage for easy seduction! "Don't worry about it." He looked down at his clothes, no longer dusty but now stiff from dried seawater. "A night beneath the stars is just what I needed."

She bit her lip. "Still, I feel badly. No more sleeping

outside, all right? Come inside. I've made you some breakfast."

"You did?" He paused, then added dryly, "Is that supposed to be consolation, or punishment?"

"I know how to cook!" she said, sticking out her tongue. "The spaghetti was not my fault. I thought the rice noodles would work."

He could feel the warmth off her body as he looked down at her. The smile slid from her face as their eyes locked, burning through him.

"Are you sure you can trust me?" he said roughly. "To be alone with you in the cottage?"

Looking up with big eyes, she nodded.

"How do you know?"

"I can feel it. Besides—" she suddenly gave him a cheeky grin "—you gave me a promise."

She headed toward the cottage. He stared at her for a moment, then followed her, admiring the sweet curve of her backside with every step. She was starting to fill out a bit, he noticed with satisfaction. He would enjoy continuing to fatten her up. He had the sudden image of Rose, rounded and pregnant with his child.

Oh, my God. Sucking in his breath, he stopped in place, nearly slapping himself on the skull. What the hell madness was this?

"This way," she called. He hurried through the cottage, barely noticing the perfectly swept floors and gleaming kitchen as he hurried past the bedroom door and out onto the lanai. The shadowed patio was still cool in the early morning. He saw she'd set up the little table for two. Next to the coffeepot was a plate with buttered toast and a carefully cut bowl of fruit beside the flowers.

She gave him a grin. "See? I know how to cook."

"Fruit and toast?"

"I wanted Mrs. Vadi to stay home until her daughter was well." She looked at him anxiously. "That's all right, isn't it? This is what I know how to make." She gave a sudden giggle. "I know I'm a wretched cook, but I'm actually much better at cleaning than cooking. The cottage looked clean, didn't it?"

He dimly remembered seeing polished floors and an immaculate kitchen. He hadn't really noticed. He never really saw the work of servants or employees, he just took the results of their labor for granted. He slowly looked at her.

"This is your idea of a vacation?" He brushed a tendril from her face. "I've never met anyone like you, Rose. The way you care so much for other people. The way you try so hard to make everyone else's life better. You never think of yourself. We're so different. So very different."

He heard her intake of breath. She tilted her head, looking up at him. "We're not."

Immediate defiance, typical of her. It almost made him choke a laugh. But he couldn't. How could she believe he had anything good in his soul?

Because she is a fool. Something he would prove to her when he seduced her, luring her into his bed for the express purpose of his own selfish pleasure, coupled with the satisfaction of causing his enemy pain. And then he would trade her.

She reached her hand up toward his rough cheek.

"You are a good man. I know you are." Her eyes were luminous as she whispered, "Why do you do it, Xerxes? Why do you pretend to have no heart?"

Her gentle touch burned him. Suddenly, he couldn't bear it. He jerked his head away from her hand.

She stared at him in surprise. He was equally surprised. This was the same strange reaction his body had had last night.

You deserve better than a man like me.

Xerxes Novros, who'd fought tycoons, ruthless despots and corrupt businessmen, had been rendered powerless by this beautiful, gentle-hearted woman.

"Excuse me," he muttered, backing away. "I need to—need to…take a shower." He glanced down again at the table, at all the effort she'd clearly put into breakfast. She must have been up before dawn to arrange the flowers and cut the fruit; doing everything herself so that the housekeeper could be home with her sick child and working hard so that he, Xerxes, would not be disappointed or angry. "I'll be back," he choked out.

Fleeing to the bathroom, he took a very hot shower, but it did not help him relax. So he turned the temperature to freezing cold. But even an arctic blast of cold water couldn't stop this fire inside him. *This fire for her.*

She was the first, the only, pure-hearted woman he'd ever known. Who would give up their own sleep, to work for free in place of a stranger who claimed to have a sick child?

Xerxes would not have done it. He didn't know anyone who would. He would have either assumed the woman was lying about the child—working some angle—or else he would have not wanted to get involved. *Not my problem*, he would have said.

And yet Rose had immediately said, *Yes, I want to help. Sick child? I'll do all your work. Go home to your daughter!*

Xerxes leaned his head against the cool marble of the shower, then turned off the water. He got dressed in khaki shorts and a snug black T-shirt.

He threw a tortured glance toward the lanai where she waited. Yes, he was hungry. But not for food.

He took a deep breath. Could he ruthlessly seduce a woman like this—a woman with such a kind soul that she believed the best of everyone, even him?

She's not some innocent virgin, his lust argued. He would make sure she thoroughly enjoyed their affair. She would have nothing to regret.

And yet he knew she would. A woman like Rose didn't take lovers easily. She couldn't have done. She wasn't jaded enough. If he took her to bed, she wouldn't just give him her body; she might give him her heart.

But he wanted her. She would be with him for days, maybe longer. How would he keep himself from taking her? He didn't have any practice at resisting desire. This was the first time he'd ever tried *not* to seduce a woman. And he'd never felt a longing as powerful as this. Need for her gripped him, body and soul.

Squaring his shoulders, he went back out on the lanai. Still waiting, Rose looked up at him, looking so innocent and fresh and pretty that a tremble went through him at the thought of defiling her.

"You must be starving." Smiling, she indicated a chair. "Coffee or tea?"

He fell heavily into his chair. "Coffee."

"Cream or…?"

"Black," he bit out.

Sitting in the chair beside him, poised as a Victorian lady, she gracefully poured coffee into his china cup. He grabbed it from her with a meaty fist and gulped down the hot black liquid, burning his tongue.

The pain was a welcome distraction. He knew how to deal with pain. What he did not comprehend was how to deal with his desire for her.

Rose stared at him in consternation, then cleared her throat. "I'm sorry."

"For what?"

She licked her lips, and he could not look away from the vision of her moist pink tongue sliding over her full lower lip, darting to the corners of her mouth. "For chasing you out of your bed last night."

Yes, she was to blame. But not in the way she thought. He raked his hand through his wet black hair, then shoved his coffee cup toward her on the table.

"More," he growled. Then at her expression, he amended, "If you please."

She poured steaming coffee from the silver coffeepot, looking impossibly lovely and old-fashioned. She was the kind of woman, Xerxes thought, that any man would want to come home to. She was the kind of woman who *made* a home.

Christ, what was he thinking? First he'd had images of her pregnant, now he was having ideas of coming home to her? He took another burning gulp of steaming hot coffee.

He was meant to be alone. He clenched his fingers

over the china cup. He always had been and always would be. Hadn't he learned that by now?

"Would you care for jam on your toast?" she asked him, holding out a tray with a smile.

"I want it plain." Taking the closest piece, he shoved it into his mouth. He barely tasted it as he ripped through it with his teeth and gulped it down, wolflike.

An awkward silence fell between them. The only sound was the caw of seagulls and the pounding surf.

"So." She took a deep breath. "Have you heard from Lars?"

"No," he bit out. It reminded him that now he would have to trade Rose to the bastard as planned, because he hadn't found Laetitia on his own. Once again, he'd been too late to reach her. Too late and too slow. And so he'd have to trade.

At the thought of giving Rose to any other man, Xerxes was so enraged he wanted to punch a wall. Instead, he shoved another piece of toast into his mouth.

"You must be starving," she murmured, trying not to stare.

Xerxes wiped his mouth with his hand, staring back at her. At the pulse of her swanlike neck. At the shape of her breasts beneath the thin eyelet lace cover-up. At the curve of her slender waist. From this close space, he could smell the scent of her, like flowers and sunshine. Her hair was long and golden and wavy. Natural. As if she'd just come from making love.

As if, instead of taking a shower, he'd cleared the breakfast table with a rough swing of his arm. As if he'd ripped off her clothes and thrown her against the bare table, kissing her neck as he thrust himself inside her.

He had to resist. For once in his life, he had to do the right thing for someone else. He couldn't seduce a woman like Rose, knowing that it would ultimately hurt her—knowing he'd still be forced to trade her back to Växborg like a used toy.

He had to resist. But still, even knowing this, his body shuddered with the effort it took not to seize her and take her like an animal, right there on the table. He took a deep breath, forcing himself to put down the remaining bits of toast he hadn't devoured. Forcing himself to pretend, for just an instant, that he was a civilized man.

"Växborg is in Las Vegas. He will contact me as soon as the divorce is final," he ground out. "I expect within days."

She blinked. "A divorce can go through so fast? Even in Las Vegas?"

"An uncontested divorce in Las Vegas usually takes about two weeks. I'm using my influence to make it go more smoothly."

"How?"

"My people are persuading every office to make this case a priority and move it to the top of the pile. It's not difficult."

"Of course it's not—for you." Looking away, she took a small sip of her creamy coffee, holding the delicate cup with light grace. "You must be desperate to see her."

Desperate was the right word, but he did not wish to be reminded of his latest failure. "And you?" he said bitterly. "Are you desperate to be back in Växborg's arms?"

She whirled back toward him, her blue-green eyes widening in shock. "You know I am not!"

He knew that, but Rose believed the best of people. Could she, in time, grow to forgive the baron as well? The thought made him cruel.

"You should know," he said brutally, "that you were not the first woman he took as his lover since his marriage."

She licked her lips. "I wasn't?"

"He's had five or six."

She set her coffee cup down on the table with a trembling hand. "You must think I'm the biggest idiot in the world," she whispered, blinking fast. "Believing Lars would actually marry anybody like me."

Staring at her, Xerxes abruptly grabbed both of her hands in his own. The sizzle of her soft touch, of her fingers against his rough palm, was torture. Ignoring the pain of his own longing, he looked into her beautiful face.

"*Anybody*? You weren't just anybody. You were the special one." His fingers tightened over hers as he whispered, "You were the only one he wanted to keep."

As if his touch burned her, she ripped her hands from his grasp, looking away.

"I still don't understand what he was doing in San Francisco when we met. He told me that he'd been looking for business opportunities—" she gave a small laugh "—but I've never seen him work."

Xerxes set his jaw, fighting the fury that threatened to choke him at the memory. "There's a medical clinic an hour east of San Francisco, the best brain trauma hospital in the world. At first I thought he'd taken Laetitia there. Instead, he dumped her at an old cabin in the mountains before he went to San Francisco to try to put her family's mansion up for sale."

Rose blinked. "A cabin?"

"It's old and desolate. No electricity. No running water." Grimly, he looked away. "When I arrived, I found dying embers in the fireplace, a new blanket on the floor, an open bag of potato chips in the kitchen. But Laetitia was gone. Since then, I've chased rumors of her around the world, looking in one desolate clinic after another, trying to find her before Lars finally gets his wish and she dies."

"I still can't believe he would be so cruel."

"You can't?" He gave a hard, ugly laugh. "Love brings out the worst kind of self-deception."

Rose's turquoise eyes looked close to tears as she sucked in her breath. "You can't still think I love him!"

He shrugged.

"What happened to you?" she said softly. "What made you so hard and cynical?"

"I just know that when people think they're in *love*—" he couldn't keep the sneer out of his voice "—they're usually lying. Either to others, or to themselves."

She blinked at him. "And yet you say you love her."

Clenching his jaw, Xerxes looked away. "I won't abandon her. I won't leave her to die alone and be forgotten. I can't. I won't."

He could see the questions in her eyes. Her body leaned toward him. But he wouldn't allow her to get any closer. His need for her already made him too vulnerable. He could not imagine what would happen if he wanted more than just her body. If he started wanting part of her heart. If he someday wanted to actually be the good man she thought he was.

Clenching his jaw, he looked down at her.

"Laetitia was barely eighteen when Växborg married her in Las Vegas. They must have argued because she was driving back alone. My guess is that she'd already decided to leave him. Then she crashed in the desert." His hands tightened. "For a year, I've tried to find her. But I feel like I'm running out of time."

His voice choked. He looked away.

Suddenly, he felt Rose's soft arms around him. She'd risen from her chair and now knelt before him, pulling him into her embrace without a word.

For a moment, he breathed in the scent of flowers and sunshine. He felt comforted. He felt safe, even protected. But that was ridiculous. He'd never been protected by anyone. So how could he feel so safe in the arms of this woman who was a foot shorter and half his body weight, who had no money in her bank account and no power of her own?

Except that was a lie. Rose had incredible power, a strength he'd never seen before. She made him betray himself from within. She tempted him beyond measure. Not just with her body or beauty or strength.

She made him feel…like he was *home*.

With an intake of breath, he closed his eyes.

"You once said everything and everyone could be bought," she said.

His eyes flew open. "Yes."

"So why not just pay Lars off, allow him to keep Laetitia's fortune?"

"Reward him for what he's done to her?" he demanded fiercely. "Allow him to profit for nearly killing her?"

Her eyes met his. "It would be the easiest thing to do."

"I do not care about *easiest*. I care about *right*. He will not receive a single euro from me. Ever," he bit out.

"Just as I thought," she said with a tremulous smile. "A man of principle. But there's one small problem."

"And that is?"

She took a deep breath. "What if Lars changes his mind about giving up everything for me?"

Xerxes reached out to stroke her cheek. "He won't. A man would do anything to possess a woman like you," he whispered. "He would betray his own soul."

She held her breath.

He started to lean toward her. Then he stopped himself, clenching his hands to his fists.

Abruptly, he rose to his feet. "I should go."

She grabbed his arm.

"Stay," she said, looking up at him.

"If I stay," he said in a low voice, "I will kiss you."

"I know."

He looked down at her harshly. "Do you know what you're asking me?"

"Yes." She looked up at him, her turquoise eyes full of light as she whispered, "I want you to kiss me."

CHAPTER ELEVEN

ROSE heard his harsh intake of breath. It was all she could do to not to release his arm. Heat suffused her cheeks at her bold words.

But she'd said it. She'd actually said the thought that had been pounding in her heart all night as she lay alone in the large bed. The question that had built inside her all morning as she made breakfast.

She'd realized Xerxes would never go back on his word not to kiss her. If she wanted him, she would have to beg.

He turned to her now, cradling her face in his strong hands as he looked down at her with such hot intensity that she felt lost in it.

"If I kiss you," he ground out, "it won't stop at a kiss."

Wouldn't it? She hadn't thought that far ahead. All she knew was that if he didn't kiss her soon, she thought she would die.

This is madness, Rose's mind was frantically trying to tell her. But her body had long stopped listening to her brain.

"It will destroy your relationship with Växborg forever," he said quietly.

Her eyes widened as she demanded, "Do you honestly think I care about that?"

"I hope not. I hope it like hell," Xerxes said roughly. Stroking her cheekbones with the pads of his thumbs, he searched her gaze with his own. "But…I want you to understand. There would be no going back."

She could see the hunger in his dark eyes, hear the ragged edge of his voice. She could feel how much he wanted her with each stroke of his trembling fingertips against her skin. Shivers of longing curled down her body, to her earlobes, down her throat, to her breasts and other sensitive places deep inside her.

"Kiss me," she whispered.

Closing her eyes, she waited, her lips parted. A warm wind blew against her skin over her thin white cover-up.

She knew an affair between them could not last. But if she never found a man she could truly love, she didn't want to die without knowing a single instant of pleasure.

She didn't need forever. She just needed today.

Or at least that was what she told herself with Xerxes so close to her that she could breathe his breath, that she could feel the warmth of his body against hers.

She felt his thumb lightly trace her sensitized lower lip.

"The pain of his betrayal is still fresh in your heart," he said in a low voice. "You want to take revenge."

Right now, Lars was the furthest thing from her mind. But opening her eyes, she saw his watchful, searching gaze. "Wouldn't you want revenge if someone betrayed you?"

"Yes," he said instantly. Then he shook his head. "But you're different. You care about people. You have a good heart. Committing an act of revenge would hurt you. And…I don't want to hurt you."

"You won't. You can't. I will never go back to him."

"You think that now," he said softly, stroking her cheek as he looked down at her with longing. "Christ, I cannot believe I am trying to talk you out of this, but… you cannot have had many lovers. Forgive me, but you are not jaded enough. You would not *have sex*, like I do. When you go to bed with someone," he said lightly, "I fear you make love with all your heart."

She choked out a laugh. "I have no idea. It's all still hypothetical."

Xerxes went very still. "What?"

This was humiliating. Her cheeks went red-hot, but he had to know. "You're going to laugh."

He did not look as if he were at all tempted to laugh. His black eyes were wide. The lanai was utterly silent except for the sound of the seagulls flying over the beach. "What do you mean, *you have no idea*?"

"It will sound stupid to a man like you."

Uncertainty filled his dark eyes as he frowned, tilting his head. "But Rose. You can't possibly mean…"

His voice trailed off. She took a deep breath and forced herself to speak the words out loud.

"I'm a virgin."

He stared at her.

"But you can't be," he whispered. "You're the most beautiful woman I've ever seen."

"And it's even worse than that." She took a deep breath. "You're the first man who's ever really kissed me."

With a gasp, he grabbed her by the shoulders, searching her eyes. His handsome face was a picture of shock. "No."

"That's why Lars threw me a fake wedding," she choked out. "Because I wouldn't kiss him. I barely let him peck my cheek at our wedding ceremony. He knew I was saving myself for my wedding night."

"And now?" he demanded, his hands gripping her shoulders painfully.

She lifted her chin. "Now I want you to kiss me."

For a moment, he stared at her. Then he exhaled with a flare of nostril. "Do not offer yourself to me out of revenge," he ground out. "Do not!"

"I'm not!"

Xerxes looked down at her. "You told me you want a love that lasts forever. And it wouldn't be forever with me. I am not the sort of man you bring home, settle down with, the man who'll marry you!"

"I don't care."

His hands tightened on her shoulders. "Don't you understand?" he said harshly. *"I will still trade you."*

"I know."

"So what the hell are you thinking?"

She took a deep breath.

"I'm tired of waiting," she whispered, "for a husband I can't find. A man who might not even exist. I want to know what it feels like to *live*. Here. Now." She faltered. "Unless…unless you don't want me after all."

Raking back his dark hair, he cursed under his breath.

"You said you love Laetitia," she continued in a small voice. "Loving her, you might be too honorable to ever let a flirtation get out of hand by betraying her—"

He grabbed her.

"I am *not* honorable," he bit out. "And you've got it all wrong. Laetitia is not my lover and she never was."

She sucked in her breath. "She's not?"

When he spoke, every word was weighed and grudging, pulled from him like blood from a stone. "My feelings…for Laetitia are more…familial…in nature."

"Familial?" She sucked in her breath. "Like how?"

He didn't answer.

"Is she your cousin? Your niece?" She bit her lip. "Surely she's not young enough to be your…your daughter?"

Clenching his jaw, he looked away.

"You aren't going to tell me, are you?"

"No," he bit out.

"Because you promised her you wouldn't?"

He gave a single unsteady nod.

Familial. So she wasn't his mistress. She wasn't his lover. Laetitia was a member of his family, or at least that was how he felt toward her.

Rose's heart suddenly lightened. She took a deep breath. She looked up at him.

"You also promised," she said softly, reaching up to stroke his face, "that you would kiss me if I begged you."

Looking down at her, he sucked in his breath.

"I'm begging you." She let her hand slowly trail down his bare throat, placing her palm against his shirt, over the rapid beat of his heart. "Kiss me. Kiss me now."

She heard him gasp, then he grabbed her hands in his own. "All right," he rasped. His voice was raw. "All right."

"All right?"

"God help me—" He crushed his mouth against hers, hard and hungry. Cradling the back of her head, he shoved her against the wall, kissing her so deeply that she nearly gasped from the exquisite, anguished pleasure. She felt his hardness against her, felt his body so much stronger and more powerful than her own. But she was no longer afraid. She kissed him back, her hands gripping his hair as she gasped for breath, tilting back her throat.

He kissed down her neck, his hands moving over her thin cover-up, murmuring words of desire that she could not hear clearly, but she still heard them ringing through her body. Cupping her breasts with his hands, he bit the edge of her throat and shoulder, causing sparks of fire to spread down her body, making her shiver and shake.

With a ragged gasp, he pulled away, abruptly meeting her gaze. "You're cold."

Without waiting for a reply, he lifted her up against his chest, carrying her from the shadows of the cool lanai out into the sun. She blinked at the intensity of the blinding light glaring off the white sand. He set her down on the warm sand of the beach, lying down beside her.

She looked up at him, dazed with emotion and sensuality. His face was in shadow, his dark head haloed by the sun, bathed in golden light.

Lowering his head, he kissed her, covering her with his body. As he ran his hands over her thin cover-up and the bare skin of her arms, she felt the weight of his body over hers and was suddenly flushed with heat.

Leaning back on his haunches, he lifted his muscular arms and pulled off his black T-shirt. Dropping it to the sand, he reached for the belt of her cover-up.

She put her hand over his. "No," she gasped. "We can't. Not out here."

"Here," he said.

"But—"

"This place is ours."

He kissed her, and his lips were so persuasive, moving against hers with aching sweetness as his tongue flicked against the corners of her lips, she could deny him nothing. She meekly submitted to his demand, barely noticing as he undid the belt of her thin cotton cover-up and pulled it off her body.

His hands moved over her bikini, beneath the tiny squares of fabric, cupping her breasts, rolling her aching nipples between his fingers. Locking his eyes with hers, he reached for the strings of her bikini and pulled them open.

She realized she was naked before him, lying on the sand. The heat of his gaze was too intense, and as he reached for his own shorts she squeezed her eyes shut. She felt the hot sun against her naked body, the sprinkle of cool mist from the pounding surf.

Then she felt his naked body over hers. He was so hard, so masculine, with muscular legs that were rough with coarse hair. His knee pushed between her thighs, separating them as he kissed her. She could feel him pressed between her legs, hard and huge, as he cupped her breasts with his hands. He suckled first one nipple, then the other, teasing with his tongue until she gasped with agonized pleasure.

Slowly, he kissed down her body. He licked her belly with tiny swirls of his tongue, flicking inside her belly button as he held her hips down with his large hands. He lowered himself farther down her body, spreading her thighs apart.

Her pulse was a rush of blood in her ears, louder than the cries of seagulls or the waving fronds of palm trees sighing against the sky above.

His breath was hot between her legs. It was shocking, wicked, but she could not fight him. Her body was his. Her head was spinning. She stretched her hands out on the sand, desperate to hold on to something, anything, to keep her body from flying off the earth and into the sky. She felt his hands move on her skin between her thighs. He couldn't be thinking…he couldn't…

Spreading her wide, he took a long taste of her with the full width of his tongue.

With a gasp, she arched off the sand. The sensation of pleasure from this intimate, forbidden act was an assault of pleasure against her body. He moved in a swirling dance, working her most sensitive spot with his tongue. Lightly, then firmly, then lightly twisting again.

Tension coiled deep inside her as her breath came in increasingly hoarse gasps. Her vision was going dark from the stars in her eyes.

"Look at me," he whispered.

She couldn't.

"Look at me," he demanded, and she had no choice but to obey.

The image of his dark head nestled between her

thighs, looking up at her, as she saw his face against her naked body, caused a surge of electricity to sizzle through her body. Her hips lifted off the sand.

Then he rose to his knees, and she got her first full look at his naked body.

Xerxes was breathtaking. Beautiful, in the strength of his muscled form and shape, in the stretch of dark hair tracing down his hard-bodied chest to his taut, flat belly and his lean hips. She saw the hard, enormous, jutting evidence of his desire for her and squeezed her eyes shut, suddenly afraid.

He covered her with his body, reaching across to gently brush tendrils of hair from her face. "Don't be afraid."

Rose kept her eyes shut. "I know it's going to hurt," she whispered. "Please just make it quick."

His low laugh made her eyes fly open. She found him looking down at her with dancing dark eyes.

"Oh, my beautiful girl," he said. "Quick is the last thing I'm going to be." As he slowly inched his way back down her body, she heard him mutter, "Even if it kills me."

He moved his head back between her legs and breathed against her. Holding her hips firmly, he pressed his mouth against the wet spot between her thighs. The pleasure was too intense, causing her hips to buck as she tried to jerk away, but he would not release her.

Feeling his tongue work her body like an instrument, playing her at his own rhythm, she was completely under his mastery and control. She could do nothing but surrender to a building joy so exquisite that it was agony as he tortured her with his sweet mouth, tossing her back and forth against the warm, white sand like a ship upon a raging sea. She heard the roar of the nearby surf as he suckled her taut center, licking and swirling her sensitive peak.

Then he pushed his tongue inside her body.

She gasped as the jolt went through her. The feeling of his hard, wet tongue inside her was like nothing she'd ever felt before. She arched her back as his tongue moved upward, slowly savoring every slippery crevice of her body. He lapped her taut center and suddenly she felt his thick finger inside her. Even as she gasped, he pulled his finger back, only to replace it with two long, wide fingers from his large hand. Stretching her. Filling her.

All the while, his hot tongue swirled incessantly against her sensitized nub, until the sensation was such sharp, sweet agony that she whimpered, begging for release, begging him to stop this torment.

But he was merciless. Holding her firmly against the sand, he began to tease her, going from full laps of his tongue to tiny swirling licks with the tip that now tantalized, but didn't touch, the taut center of her longing. And when she could bear it no longer, when her gasping breath had shrunk her vision of the blue sky to small pinpricks in a sea of black, he suckled and bit her sensitive nub at the same moment he thrust three fingers inside her, bursting her into a thousand pieces. Rose screamed as her world exploded.

Instantly, he lifted his mouth from her, shoving her legs apart with his hips, positioning his hardness between her thighs. She was still gasping for breath, lost in dazed ecstasy, when she felt his hardness pressing against her wet core, demanding entrance.

With a ragged breath, he pushed himself inside her with one relentless movement.

She was unprepared for the shock of pain, unready for the enormous size of him entering her virgin body, as he pushed himself inside her. She choked back a cry.

He froze, holding himself utterly still.

Then slowly, as she exhaled, he began to move inside her. Gently, ever so gently, he swayed his hips against her, rocking back and forth as he thrust with agonizing slowness inside her. To her surprise, a new wave of pleasure begin to build, coiling low in her belly. A new shot of ecstasy swept her up almost instantly as he filled her so deeply and completely, all the way to her heart.

Deeper. *Deeper.* His force split her in two but the pain had somehow turned into hot, molten pleasure. It built so hard and fast that within minutes, she gasped out his name as she felt a second explosion, even deeper and more shattering than the first, and she screamed. His deep, low voice joined her, shouting out his pleasure with a growl of ecstasy, and she felt tears on her cheeks and realized she was weeping with joy.

After Xerxes collapsed over her sweet naked body, it took a long time before he slowly came back to his senses.

Eventually, he felt the hot sun on his back, felt the rough sand against his knees. He looked down at the beautiful woman in his arms. Her eyes were closed, her lips curved in a smile.

His heart turned over in his chest.

He'd never felt anything like this. Ever. For anyone.

He'd never even imagined lovemaking could feel like this. Was it because he'd never taken a virgin to his bed before? Was that why he felt such amazement, such tenderness?

It had nearly killed him to hold himself back as he'd made love to her. But knowing she was a virgin, he'd wanted to make it good for her. And what she'd done for him…the way she'd made him feel…

Tenderly, he rolled off her body so he wouldn't crush her with his weight. He moved to her side, still cradling her body with his own. He'd wanted nothing more than to make love to her like this, on the white sand as the waves crashed beneath the palm trees. He'd wanted to fill her, to impale her, to make her scream out his name. But it hadn't been like he'd imagined. It had been better. It had been the single most amazing sexual experience of his life.

Tucking his hand behind his head, he stared up at the wispy white clouds drifting over the blue sky. Then he glanced at the beautiful woman in his arms, and realized to his shock that he already wanted more of her. And it was even more shocking than that.

He realized in that moment that he didn't want to give her up. Ever. He wanted to possess her forever.

CHAPTER TWELVE

THE next morning, Rose lay cradled against him in the large bed as she stared out the bedroom window, watching the pink streaks of sunrise cross the sky.

They'd moved into the bedroom sometime yesterday afternoon. They'd spent the rest of the night there, only leaving the bed to shower and scavenge and devour simple meals in the kitchen.

She looked at him now as he slept. His peaceful face looked younger somehow, almost boyish. Sleeping with him all night, in his arms after the many times they'd made love, was utter bliss. It was exquisite.

It was torture.

Why did she feel this way—so completely infatuated, so enamored, so connected to him in every way possible? Was it because he'd taken her virginity? Was she deluding herself, like she had with Lars, into imagining Xerxes as the fulfillment of some romantic dream?

"Don't think I'm a good person," he'd told her grimly. She didn't want to believe him. How could she when every inch of her body down to blood and bone insisted differently? And Xerxes had kept every promise he'd made to her. Even last night, when she'd practically thrown herself at him, he'd actually tried to let her go,

to warn her off. She was the one who'd called him on his promise, demanding that he kiss her. Giving him her virginity had been entirely her choice.

She didn't regret it. She couldn't.

And yet...

She'd told herself she could just have casual sex—that she could experience sensual pleasure without falling in love. Now, she realized how foolish she had truly been to think she could ever keep her heart separate from her body. She did not have the walls of armor that men had. That Xerxes had.

"No regrets?" he said quietly beside her, as if he'd read her mind.

She turned to him with an unsteady smile. "None," she lied, her heart in her throat. "In fact, I was just thinking I should have jumped into bed with some man a long time ago."

He growled. "I am glad you did not."

Leaning forward, he kissed her. His embrace was tender, making her heart yearn and twist and break beneath the pleasure.

He pulled back, his dark brows lowered in concern as he searched her gaze. "What's wrong, Rose?" he said quietly. "Are you thinking of Växborg?"

"No."

"You still love him."

"*No.*" She shook her head fiercely. "I don't think I ever did."

He looked at her, his dark eyes shining. "I am glad."

Their eyes locked, and for a moment, she was utterly lost. Her memory of Lars seemed like a dewdrop compared to the ocean of longing and desire she felt for Xerxes now.

But she couldn't fall in love with Xerxes after he'd specifically warned her not to! She couldn't be that stupid—that *gullible and naive!*

Abruptly, she sat up in bed.

"Rose?"

"I'm fine." She smiled back at him, but it took an effort. She blinked fast to hide threatening tears. "I'm great. We had a fun night together. It's no big deal."

"It was your first time," he said softly, putting his hands below his head on the pillow. He smiled, his eyes caressing her. "Of course it's a big deal."

"Well, you needn't worry." She looked away. "I'm not going to pester you for an engagement ring."

"That's good," he said with a snort. "We both know I am not the sort of man for you to bring home to your parents. I'm not exactly husband-and-father material."

"Right."

"I mean it." He sat up beside her, his eyes suddenly serious. "You think Växborg is a selfish bastard? I am worse."

She looked away. "So you say."

"I'm no good to any woman," he insisted. "Least of all a woman like you. Rose…" Reaching out, he took her hands in his larger ones. "You deserve the fairy tale. And we both know I am no white knight."

She pulled her hands away.

"Honestly, you don't need to explain." Her voice cracked. "I'm fine. In a few days, you can trade me and I'll go back home to California and find a man I can truly love. Someone who's honorable, kind and strong. A man I can love for the rest of my life."

Silence fell.

"And if he never comes?" Xerxes said quietly.

The thought caused pain in her throat. "Then I'll be alone," she whispered. "Until the day that I die."

"That won't happen." He pulled her back into his arms. She tried to resist, but he was inexorable. He held her against his naked chest for long moments, as they watched the sky outside grow bluer and brighter. "You will have a happy life. You'll see. You will. You must."

Still cradled against his chest, she looked back at him. Their eyes locked as, with agonizing slowness, he lowered his mouth to hers.

"You deserve everything good in this world," he whispered against her skin. She felt his hands stroking her, felt his fingers twisting in her tangled hair before he kissed her. After the intense passion of the previous night, he was gentle now, tender against her bruised lips. His kiss was so poignant and sweet that tears burned her eyes. She felt choked with emotion.

Why did her heart ache like this? Was it just the overflow of too much passion, too much joy in his arms? Or was it the pain of knowing it would not last?

His kiss deepened. Rolling back on the mattress, he lifted her over him, stroking her naked back, making her shiver in the cool dawn. Looking down at him beneath her on the bed, Rose thought she'd never seen a man at once so beautiful and brutal. His jaw was rough and unshaven, his short black hair mussed from all their hours of lovemaking. His body was tanned and muscular, from his broad shoulders to his taut belly to his thighs thick as tree trunks.

Xerxes was like no man she'd ever met. If he wasn't a white knight, then he was the dark prince of midnight dreams.

He left her breathless. His strength. His power. Most of all, the dark heat in his eyes as he looked up at her.

His hands lifted up her hips. As if she weighed nothing at all, he lowered her with exquisite slowness, impaling her, causing them both to gasp as he filled her inch by inch. Rose tossed back her head, exposing her neck as her eyes rolled back with the pleasure. He guided her, allowing her to establish her own rhythm, teaching her to ride him. Tension coiled inside her deep and fast, and when she finally exploded, she screamed. He plunged inside her with a final deep thrust, shouting her name with a bestial growl that somehow sounded like a prayer. When she collapsed over his body, utterly spent, it took ten minutes before she stopped shaking.

Afterward, as they slept in each other's arms, Rose opened her eyes to stare blankly at the brilliant sunlight on the ocean.

She could no longer deny her feelings.

Xerxes had seen her at her worst. And he'd accepted her, just as she was. Perhaps because he accepted himself. He knew he wasn't perfect, so she didn't need to be, either. They could both have faults, but still be... friends.

Friends?

Friendship did not describe the longing of her heart.

But what she felt could only bring pain. Even if

Xerxes cared about her, he would still trade her for Laetitia. In a heartbeat.

"My feelings for Laetitia are more familial in nature," he'd said. Could she be his cousin? His niece? The daughter of an old friend? Who? Rose wished she knew.

But one thing she did know for sure: Xerxes Novros always kept his promises. And in spite of his best warnings, when she'd given him her body, she'd also given him her heart.

Outside, the sunshine was brilliant and bright, and the morning birds sang sweetly in the blue sky. And Rose silently wept in his arms as he slept.

She was in love with Xerxes. And she knew there was only one way it could end. With her own broken heart.

Xerxes was awakened from a very pleasant dream by a persistent buzzing and rattling sound against the hard tile floor. Blearily, he opened his eyes and saw his cell phone vibrating in his shorts pocket next to the bed. He glanced at Rose, hoping it hadn't woken her. It hadn't. A smile traced his lips at how peacefully she slept, his kittenish beauty.

Careful not to jostle her—they'd gotten so little sleep, it would be cruel to wake her for anything but sex—he climbed out of bed and carried the phone outside the bedroom, closing the door softly behind him. "Novros."

"This time we've found her, boss," his chief bodyguard said tersely. "Montez is sure."

Ten minutes later, Xerxes was shaved, showered and

dressed. He returned to the bedroom filled with nervous energy. His hand reached out to shake Rose's shoulder and awaken her, then he paused, looking down at her.

He could still hardly believe she'd been a virgin before yesterday. And that she'd deliberately chosen him, of all men on earth, to be her first lover. He shivered, remembering all the times they'd made love in the last twenty-four hours. He should have been satiated, but looking at her now, he very nearly forgot his mission and climbed back into bed.

Then he stopped himself. No. He had a lead on Laetitia and couldn't blow it. He had to focus. If he could find Laetitia, he could save her.

And then he could keep Rose for himself.

If he could really be that selfish to keep her, knowing she would be better off with a better man, instead of with a ruthless, heartless bastard like him.

Xerxes looked down at her, and his whole body hardened. Yes, he thought grimly. He could be that selfish. At this moment, he would kill any man who tried to take her away from him.

Reaching out, he lightly shook Rose's shoulder. "Wake up," he said in a low voice. "We need to go."

"Go?" She yawned, stretching her body across the bed, from her hands to her toes. "Go where?"

The sheet had fallen from her body, leaving her upper body bare. His back broke out in a hot sweat at the sight of those lusciously full breasts, the pink tips that he'd suckled just hours before, cupping them in his hands as he… Xerxes shuddered.

Forcefully, he made himself look away from her, before he forgot such minor details like promises and honor and jumped into bed with her for another twenty-four hours. Clenching his hands into fists, he forced himself not to touch her, to have some self-control. "Mexico."

"Mexico?" She sounded bewildered. "Why? Do you have business there?"

He cleared his throat, unwilling to explain. "In a manner of speaking. Get dressed. My assistant is already packing your bikinis. And the rest of your wardrobe."

"What wardrobe?" she demanded. "I only have bikinis thanks to you!"

"I might have sent away for more clothes."

"When was that?"

"A few hours after we arrived."

"Why didn't you tell me?" Her furious voice ended with a squeak that made him grin. He almost turned to look at her, then stopped himself just in time before he got another image of her sprawled naked across the bed. Christ, he only had so much willpower—he was only a man! He hurried toward the door. "The suitcase is still packed beneath the bed. We leave in ten minutes."

But once again, his foolish hopes of finding Laetitia proved destined for failure. As soon as their jet arrived in Cabo San Lucas, he dropped Rose off without explanation at a luxury gated villa in the hills. He drove with bodyguards in an open Jeep, going north on a dirt road to the little desert village in Baja California.

At a shabby little casita, he knocked on the door. Xerxes heard a woman's low moan inside, and adrenaline ripped through his body. Shouting Laetitia's name, he kicked open the door.

He found a woman lying on a small bed, a brunette

Laetitia's size with bandages on her face. For a moment, he'd believed that after all these months, he'd finally found her.

Then he'd heard the language the woman was shouting. German? It turned out she was a wealthy businesswoman from Berlin who'd come to recover from her face-lift in privacy and seclusion. Xerxes had only convinced her not to call the police through substantial cash compensation.

Cash that would come out of his payment to Montez, Xerxes thought, gritting his teeth, for feeding his chief bodyguard such faulty information.

But in his heart Xerxes did not blame the investigator. He blamed only himself. He was the one who'd failed Laetitia, again and again over the past year. And she was still out there somewhere. Dying. Alone.

They drove back to Cabo San Lucas in silence. Entering the villa, Xerxes felt hollowed out. He walked through the heavily embellished oak door with his shoulders hunched. Wearily, he pushed open the door, and the hinges squealed like nails on a chalkboard, the harsh noise scraping his soul.

Then at that moment, he heard a miracle that soothed the pain in his heart. Rose's sweet, clear voice.

"I'm so glad you're home!"

Slowly, he looked up.

Rose stood in front of the wide sunlit veranda overlooking the Pacific, looking fresh and pretty in a new sleeveless pink dress, her blond hair tumbling down her shoulders. He exhaled. Everything good in the world seemed wrapped up in her.

She saw his bleak expression and her turquoise eyes

widened. She didn't ask any questions. She just held out her arms.

Without a word, he went to her. He nearly choked out a sob when he felt her soft arms go around him, but he held it inside. A man didn't cry. He'd learned that long ago. But there were other things a man could do.

He led her through the villa, with its soaring ceiling and colonial-style architecture. He turned on the shower, and the hot steam filled the room. Without a word, he turned to Rose and slowly unbuttoned her dress.

She did not resist. She stood before him, watching him with her heart on her expressive face. He pulled off her clothes, dropping her dress, her bra, her panties to the clay tile floor. He pulled off his own clothes. Taking her hand, he pulled her into the enormous shower.

The hot water burned him, washing off the dust and grime and sorrow. He looked down at Rose. Her petite, curvaceous body was naked, her lustrous skin pink with the heat of the steam. Tilting her head back with his hands, he washed her hair.

She submitted without a word, without complaint, without demands. Her silent sympathy healed his wounded soul as nothing else ever had. As nothing could.

Turning her around, he held her against the glass wall of the shower and lowered his mouth to hers in a hard, demanding kiss. When she returned his embrace, he did not wait. He lifted her legs around his waist. Without warning or permission, he took her as his own, thrusting inside her, holding her against the shower wall. He exploded as steam and hot water poured over them both.

Afterward, he took her to the bed and made love to her again, this time with tenderness, bringing her to gasping fulfillment that made her weep tears of joy. Who was this woman? He thought as he held her to his chest. Who was this woman who could offer him her sympathy, her body, her heart—without making any demands of her own?

He should have known it wouldn't last.

Later that night, as they were served dinner by the rented villa's housekeeper, Rose suddenly looked up at him in the candlelight. The two of them were sitting together at the end of a long table, in front of the wall of windows with a view of the moonlit Pacific and the Gulf of Cortez. He could see an old fishing boat with hanging lights, and in the distance was an enormous cruise ship. Mariachi music from the resort town below drifted up the hillside through the open windows.

Rose took a bracing gulp of a lime margarita, then leaned forward over the table. The candlelight cast shadows on her face, giving her the beautiful, concerned expression of a Renaissance Madonna as she asked quietly, "Why have we been traveling so much? Has Lars called the police? Has he been chasing us?"

Xerxes snorted. "Växborg would never call the police. That would just reveal his own crimes. He's still in Las Vegas, settling the divorce."

"Then why?" She pressed her lips together. "It must be your business making such demands," she said softly. She shook her head. "It must exhaust you."

He wanted to explain to her that it wasn't his business, just his failure to find Laetitia that kept them constantly on the move; but the words choked in his throat. He couldn't bear Rose's sympathy now, on top of everything else. If she tried to smile and tell him consolingly that he was still *a good man* and no doubt *trying his best*, or that it *wasn't his fault*, he would smash the wall with his fist.

When he did not reply, she looked down at her plate. She took another bite of her *enchiladas de mariscos*. Waving her fork, she tilted her head at him, her eyes gleaming.

"I know you're rich and powerful and all," she teased, clearly trying to elevate the mood, "but what exactly do you do, anyway?"

Xerxes served himself more of the enchiladas and fish tacos that the villa's cook had prepared. "I buy distressed companies. I sell the divisions that are profitable. I discard the parts that are not."

Her face closed down. "Oh."

He blinked at her. "You don't approve?"

She shook her head.

"Why?" he asked curiously.

She shrugged.

"Tell me."

She sighed. "Look, I know I don't have any right to criticize. You're a millionaire with a private jet and I'm a waitress with fifty dollars in my bank account. But I've been working my way through college, studying entrepreneurial business management at San Francisco State…" She hesitated, biting her lip, as if she expected him to mock her.

He leaned forward in his chair. "Go on."

"Your company seems profitable, and that's great, but…"

"Yes?"

She pressed her lips together, then looked up. "But *people* work at those companies. People who lose their jobs."

"So?"

There was a loud burst of mariachi music from the town below, and she looked in the distance at the dark, moonswept Pacific. "I'm biased, I guess. My grandfather had a candy company a long time ago. It did really well, then things fell apart. Ingredients became more expensive, and we didn't have the nationwide distribution of the larger companies. Ten years ago, after my father took over, a conglomerate offered to buy Linden Candy. It would have made us wealthy, but my dad knew they'd close the factory and move production, leaving half our town out of work. So for the sake of his employees—his neighbors and friends—my father refused."

"Foolish."

"No, not foolish!" she retorted. "It was *noble*. Courageous, even. My dad said we would either all sink together, or he would find a way to make the company succeed."

"And what happened?"

She looked down at her hands in her lap. "In spite of all his best efforts, the company went bankrupt."

Xerxes gave a single firm nod. "He never should have allowed his feelings to override his business judgment."

"He was protecting his employees!"

"He didn't protect them. He failed them. And worse— he failed you. If he'd sold the company, you wouldn't be working your way through college at the age of twenty-nine."

She glared at him. "My father did the right thing. He held to his principles. I thought you of all people would appreciate that."

"I *of all people* believe in facing reality. The company was a business. Not a charitable institution."

"You sound so harsh!"

"That is how business works," he said evenly, dipping his taco chips into his shrimp *ceviche* and fresh guacamole. "Things that were once successful die, they get replaced by the new. Business."

"It doesn't have to be that way." She bit her lip, then said in a rush, "Someday, I'll start it up again. I've made up a business plan. I'll find a way to open the factory and—"

"Forget it," he said brutally. "Accept it's over and move on."

She looked away, trembling. She took a gulp of lime margarita, then set the glass back down on the table. "It's easy for you to say, isn't it? You just break companies up for parts. Dissecting and eating them like a vulture."

"It's profitable."

"You would have no clue how to truly run a company, to love it and invest your heart and soul in it."

"You're right," he said. "And I wouldn't want to. I don't want it to be personal. It's *business.*"

"Nothing's ever personal for you, is it?" Putting her hands on the table, she pushed herself to her feet. "I feel sorry for you. I do."

If it had been anyone else, he would have shrugged off their criticism and let them leave. But not Rose.

She was the one person he couldn't stand to be angry at him.

He reached his hand over hers. "I'm sorry," he said softly. "I don't wish to fight with you."

Her eyes relented. "I don't want to fight, either." She licked her lips and said, "But if you could just see how much greater it could be, how much more satisfying and challenging, to actually create something of value, anything—"

"No," he said. "Even if I could do it, I wouldn't. It would be a waste of energy and money." He rose to his feet. "You've been cooped up in this penthouse all day. Shall we go out?"

"Out?" she said in astonishment.

He shrugged, even as his eyes caressed her. "I hear music from town. Want to go dancing with me?"

She sucked in her breath. "You would let me go out in public? You'd trust me not to run to the police?"

"If you'll give me your word you won't, I'll trust you."

"I give you my word," she said, then paused. "Anyway, I want to help Laetitia now. I...want to help you."

Of course she did, Xerxes thought, his eyes searching her sweetly beautiful face as if memorizing it for eternity. He'd kidnapped her, seduced her, refused to answer her questions. And yet she wanted to help him. Rose had the most loving heart of any woman—any person—he'd ever known.

She bit her lip, her face suddenly drawn. "But when do you think Lars will finalize the divorce?"

Xerxes didn't want to think about it. "Any day now."

She looked sad, then brightened. "But we have to-night. And I can hardly believe how much I've seen of the world in such a short time," she said as he wrapped a pale cashmere cardigan around her shoulders.

"You haven't minded all the travel?"

"Mind it?" She ticked off her fingers. "Greece, the Maldives, and now Mexico. After spending my whole life close to home, barely leaving northern California, it's been amazing!"

"That's what I can't imagine."

"Never going anywhere?"

"Having a home that I didn't wish to leave."

"You've never had a home?"

He didn't like the pity in her eyes. "I haven't needed one." He looked down at her. *But you make everywhere feel like home to me*, he thought. All he said was, "I've enjoyed our time together as well."

"I wasn't sure if you even liked me at first," she said teasingly as he escorted her from the villa toward his rented MG convertible. "When you left it up to me to decide if we would even kiss…"

As he opened her door, he said, "I always knew I would get you into bed."

She froze, then looked back at him. "You did?"

He suddenly wanted to tell her the truth. *Had* to tell her the truth. "I seduced you deliberately, Rose. Bit by bit. But I always knew I would win."

"Oh." Looking dazed, she climbed into the convert-ible and he closed the door behind her. Climbing into the driver's side, he drove them out of the gated community down the winding hillside toward town. She remained silent for a few moments. He looked at her.

"Now do you regret our affair?" he said quietly.

"No." She turned away. "It's just…"

"Just?"

"When I meet the man I marry," she said in a small voice, "what if he asks me why I didn't wait for him? What if he asks why I didn't have faith?"

"Rose!" he growled.

"But the thing is, I did wait," she whispered. "I waited so long. And he never came. The only man who seemed remotely like a prince turned out to be a massive frog."

Xerxes looked at her and envied—no, *hated*—the man she would someday marry. "He won't ask you any stupid questions like that. He'll just get down on his knees and thank God you are his wife."

She gave him a tremulous smile. "Really?"

"Yes." He found a parking spot near the marina. Turning off the car engine, he turned to face her beneath the warm lights of the town and took her hands in his own.

"I wonder if you have any idea how truly rare you are," he said. "How you make life beautiful wherever you go. To everyone around you. Even me."

She glanced at him out of the corner of her eye. He saw the emotion in her face, but her voice seemed purposefully light as she said, "Well, you were a hard case."

He snorted a laugh, but as he leaned forward to kiss her, his phone rang. He was still smiling when he answered, "Novros."

"We're divorced."

Växborg's voice was full of repressed fury.

Xerxes turned away from Rose, speaking in a low voice. "What?"

"You heard me."

"The filing is complete?"

"Yes. I've used your connections to push it through. Tomorrow morning, it will be registered as final."

"Then call me tomorrow," Xerxes said shortly, but his eyes traced over Rose, who was watching him with big eyes. *Tomorrow.* He would have to give her up so soon?

"Wait!" Växborg said. "I need to talk to Rose."

"No."

"Her father just called. Her grandmother has had a heart attack and might not last the night. You have to let me take Rose home."

"You think I'll fall for that?" Xerxes said with a snort.

"Have a heart, you bastard. It's her family!"

Xerxes looked at Rose's face, so sweet and trusting. Family meant everything to her.

His jaw hardened. "I don't have a heart, Växborg," he replied coldly. "Haven't you learned that by now?"

"Was it Lars?" Rose asked after he'd hung up.

He gave a grim nod.

"And?"

"The divorce will be final in the morning."

"Oh," she said in a small voice. He saw the tremble of her delicate swanlike throat as she said, "So tonight's our last night."

They'd both known, all along, that their affair would soon end. What he hadn't realized was how completely and utterly he would hate the thought of ever letting her go. He gave a single unsteady nod.

"You'll still trade me," she whispered. "Won't you?"

He'd made a promise. He had no choice. "Yes."

She gave him a trembling smile. "Then tonight is a celebration, I guess. Tomorrow, we'll both get what we want. I'll go home to my family, and you'll get Laetitia back."

Staring at her, Xerxes set his jaw. He abruptly turned away, dialing his phone and speaking into it in rapid Greek. When he hung up his phone, his suspicions had been confirmed. Växborg hadn't lied.

"Where shall we go first?" Rose said, visibly forcing a smile. "Shall we go dancing, as you said?"

"The airport."

"The airport?" She sucked in her breath, then sounded near tears as she said, "We can't even have one last night?"

"I'm taking you to San Francisco," he said quietly.

"San Francisco? Not Las Vegas?"

Looking down at her, he placed his hands gently over hers. "You're going to need to be strong, Rose. I have some bad news. Your grandmother's had a heart attack."

Rose gasped, falling back against her car seat. He grabbed her, cradling her against his chest.

"I'll get her the best care, Rose," he vowed. "She'll be all right. I promise you."

She stared up at him, her brow furrowed. Then she embraced him in a flood of tears.

"Thank you," she wept.

Xerxes held her to his chest, stroking her back, murmuring words of nonsensical comfort. All he could think about was that he would do anything, absolutely anything, to make her grandmother well. *Anything to make Rose happy.*

When she finally pulled away to look up at him, tears were streaming down her face. "Why are you being so good to us?" she whispered. "You don't even know her."

"No," Xerxes said quietly. Looking down at her, he stroked her beautiful face and felt a lump in his throat as he said, "But I know you love her. That's all I need to know."

CHAPTER THIRTEEN

IT WAS almost midnight when Rose finally collapsed in her old childhood bedroom.

Trembling with exhaustion, clasping the same pink cardigan she'd worn in Mexico more tightly over her arms, she sank down on her small single bed, staring blankly at old posters of rock stars she'd pasted as a teenager over the peeling, faded floral wallpaper. A beloved old teddy bear looked down from her bookshelves, next to baking trophies she'd won at the local fair in high school. Downstairs, she could hear her family talking in low voices as they moved over the creaky floorboards. She could smell her mother's clam chowder bubbling on the stove.

She was home. Nothing had changed. And yet—Rose looked at Xerxes's dark form in front of her window—everything had changed.

They'd both changed on the jet into clothes more appropriate for the cold rain of northern California. Now wearing black pants, a white shirt and a black woolen coat, he looked out at the lights twinkling in the distance. "Is that your family's old factory?"

Rose had spent most of her childhood sitting in that window, reading books and staring out dreamily at the rainy gray surf beneath the ocean cliff. She knew every view from the rambling Victorian house by heart. "Yes."

A few dim lights still illuminated the old hollow shell of her grandfather's factory, which had once employed half this small town making chewy taffies in the heyday of the 1950s and 1960s. But Rose didn't want to talk about the factory. She didn't want to hear Xerxes tell her yet again that it was a hopeless situation and she should let it go.

Instead, she wanted to breathe in this moment and just be grateful. Grateful that her grandmother had lived and was getting better. Grateful that she herself was finally home.

Crossing her ankles and tucking her black jean-clad legs beneath her, Rose looked up at him. "Thank you."

Blinking, he glanced back at her. "For what?"

"How can you even ask? For everything you did for Gran."

He shrugged. "I did nothing."

"You're wrong," she said softly. "You brought me home."

He gave her a wry smile. "Your grandmother didn't know whether to hug me or slap me, did she?"

When they'd arrived a few hours earlier, Xerxes had already summoned the top cardiologist from San Francisco to meet them at the local hospital. The doctor had run tests on her grandmother's heart and confirmed it hadn't been an actual attack, but an "episode" that was no lasting cause for concern, as long as Dorothy

Linden adjusted her diet and started getting more regular exercise.

The elderly woman, for her part, stubbornly maintained that no exercise or diet changes were necessary because she'd just had a broken heart worrying about her granddaughter.

And no wonder. Rose had discovered that Lars had explained her disappearance by telling them Rose was just a flighty, runaway bride who'd changed her mind and couldn't be bothered to contact her family. That was his big explanation!

Rose growled. If she hadn't hated Lars before, she'd have certainly hated him now. Rather than admit any of his own guilt, he'd left Rose in the position of having to explain to her grandmother—who was still in the hospital for observation, at the cardiologist's insistence—why Rose, supposedly a married woman, had disappeared for days after her wedding only to reappear here today with another man on her arm!

Thank heaven for Xerxes. He'd been her rock through all of this. Looking up now at the set of his jaw, at the hard lines of his handsome face as he stared out the window of her bedroom, Rose blinked back tears. When she'd tried to explain to her family what had happened, she'd floundered helplessly.

Then Xerxes had stepped in. He'd gently explained to her grandmother that Lars had lied, that he'd never been free to wed and that he, Xerxes, had kidnapped Rose from her own wedding to force him to admit he already had a wife. Xerxes had quietly faced down her family's wrath and blame, and told them he was sorry. He'd been kind and courteous.

The only thing he hadn't told them was that he and Rose had become lovers. Which, in this family, was probably all for the best.

Now he was in Rose's old bedroom. This handsome, powerful man, who'd been so good to her family. This devastatingly strong man who'd moved heaven and earth to bring Rose home in record time. This ruthless man who she knew had a good heart, no matter how he might try to hide it. *This man she loved.*

Looking at his dark figure in front of the window, she suddenly trembled in a way that had nothing to do with exhaustion.

"Why did you bring me home?" She rose slowly to her feet. "The local sheriff is a friend of the family. He lives just down the street."

He stared at her, and for the first time she noticed the dark circles under his eyes. "If you want to escape, or have me arrested, I know I cannot stop you now."

"So why did you do it? Why risk bringing me back here, when you knew you might lose me as a bargaining chip to get Laetitia—or worse?"

He looked down at the old hardwood floor. "Because your family means everything to you." He smiled to himself. "They're just like you said they were."

As if on cue, she heard her young nephews scuffling downstairs, heard them knock something over with a loud crash. As her father's loud scolding floated up through the floorboards, Xerxes gave a low laugh. "I never imagined a family could really be like this."

"Was your childhood so different?"

His jaw clenched as he turned back to the window. "I always knew I was neither wanted nor loved. My mother was a maid in San Francisco who got pregnant by her boss."

Her eyes widened. "You're from San Francisco?"

He shrugged. "I lived there until I was five, when my mother got fed up with responsibility. She went back to her old employer and threatened to reveal my existence to his fragile, wealthy wife." He gave a harsh laugh. "To get rid of the problem, my father paid her off, then sent me to live with my shamed grandparents in Greece."

"At five!" Rose said, shocked. "That must have broken your mother's heart!"

He snorted. "She took her payoff money and left for a life of excitement and freedom in Miami." As if examining the fabric, he ran his hand idly along her old linen curtains. "She never wanted to go back to the life she'd fled, to a barren island of rocks and parents who despised her modern ways. My grandparents did not speak English and were ashamed of me, their bastard grandson. But my *father*—" he spat out the word "—sent some money, so I was a source of income they could not refuse."

Rose stared at him, pain curling around her heart. She thought of the five-year-old boy, abandoned by his mother, rejected by his father, sent away to be ignored and despised by his grandparents in a faraway land.

Xerxes's eyes traced around Rose's old bedroom. "I used to dream of having a home like this, a family like this. When my grandparents didn't speak to me for days, I dreamed of someday coming back to America and finding my real parents."

"And did you?" she breathed.

He gave a hard, ugly laugh. "Yes. But by then I was

a grown man who'd already made my fortune. I found my father and took his business apart."

"You ruined your own father?" she whispered.

"And I enjoyed it." His eyes glittered. "I did not know he would die from the heart attack. But I should have known he had a weak heart, from the way he condemned me as a child to loneliness and silence."

"Oh, Xerxes…"

He paused. "I did keep the one secret he cared about, just out of spite. I never revealed to the world that I was his son."

"You protected him."

"He wasn't the one I was protecting." He abruptly closed the curtains, covering the window. "Then I went looking for my mother and found her in Florida, living in a rathole, abandoned by her latest lover, dying from liver disease and booze."

"What did you do?"

"I brought her a bottle of vodka in a bright red bow." He gave a hard laugh. "She was glad to see it. I'd planned to abandon her, as she had me." He looked away. "Instead, I tried to get her to go to rehab, bought her a new apartment and paid her bills until she died."

"You cared for her," Rose whispered.

He shrugged with a casual air belied by the darkness in his eyes. "A moment of weakness. And she died anyway."

Rose's heart was in her throat. Coming behind him, she wrapped her arms around him, pressing her cheek to his back. "I'm sorry."

He turned around in her arms.

"Now you know what I am," he said in a low voice.

"Now you know why you'd be a fool to love me. Even you. Especially you."

But I do, she thought, her heart aching in her chest. *I do love you.*

Her lips parted to speak the words, but at that moment her bedroom door was pushed open with a loud squeak of the hinges. Her mother stood in the doorway, wearing her usual vintage floral apron over her pantsuit. Vera Linden took one look at the couple and put her hands on her hips.

"Now, you two," she said warningly. She turned to Xerxes with a greater show of warmth. "Mr. Novros—"

"Xerxes," he corrected her with a smile.

"Xerxes, we've set you up for the night in Tom's old room down the hall. I'll show you." Her mother glanced between them sharply. "But there'll be no funny business tonight. I mean it."

"Of course not, ma'am," Xerxes said meekly. He looked at Rose, and his dark eyes danced with sudden laughter. Then he sobered. "Get some sleep, Rose. We leave for Las Vegas in the morning."

As the door closed, Rose sucked in her breath. In the morning. *The trade.*

Pushing the painful reminder away, Rose stared at the closed door as she changed into old flannel pajamas. The only thing more strange than having Xerxes in her childhood home was how well he fit in here. He blended with her family in a way that Lars never had. Lars never would have slept in her brother's old room. He would have insisted on renting a suite at a luxury seaside hotel twenty miles away. That is, if he'd even been willing to bear the inconvenience of a night here at all.

"Rose?"

She looked up to see Vera in her doorway. "Hi, Mom."

"I meant to bring this to you earlier." Her mother sat down beside her on the bed and handed her a cup of peppermint tea. "I'm so glad you're back. We were all so worried."

"Thanks." Rose took a sip of the lukewarm tea, then added in a carefully casual tone, "Is Xerxes settled in?"

Vera snorted, then shook her head wryly. "And to think just a few days ago we were in Sweden, watching you marry another man."

Rose blushed. "Yeah," she muttered. "Funny, huh?"

"I guess it's all right to tell you now that I never liked Lars, Rose."

"You didn't like him?" Rose said in surprise. "You never said so."

Her mother shrugged. "What business is it of mine whom you choose to love? But I always hoped when you finally settled down," she said wistfully, "you would bring home a man who's just regular folk, like us." She paused. "A man like the one who's sleeping right now in Tom's room down the hall."

Rose nearly snorted peppermint tea out of her nose hearing Xerxes Novros, the international Greek millionaire, described by her mother as *regular folk*.

"Anyway, thank heaven your gran is better." Her mother rose from the bed with a tender smile. "And you're home. Everything is all right now." She paused at the door, her hands on her hips as she swiveled around, her eyes narrowed. "But I meant what I said, Rosie. No funny business in our house."

"All right, Mom," Rose said, rolling her eyes. But she could see why her mother had felt the need to repeat the warning. As she walked down the hall later to brush her teeth, her feet slowed down of their own accord as she passed by her brother's old room where Xerxes slept.

She loved him. Why hadn't she told him when she had the chance? Why couldn't she be brave enough to tell him now?

After washing her face and brushing her teeth in the bathroom, she paused again at his closed door as she returned down the hall. Raising her hand to knock, she hesitated. Then with a deep breath, she rapped softly.

There was no answer.

She exhaled. He must be asleep already. She sighed, filled with a jumble of nerves and disappointment.

Tomorrow, Rose vowed to herself. She would tell him that she loved him before they reached Las Vegas. Tomorrow, before he traded her for Laetitia and her chance was lost forever.

She'd already experienced so many miracles in her life. The miracle of a good family. Of a home. Of a grandmother who was steadily getting better.

Having Xerxes love her back would be too much to ask. But tomorrow, Rose would take her courage in her hands and do it.

Xerxes heard a soft knock on his door.

Rose. She'd come to him, in spite of her mother's

warning. With an intake of breath, he hurried from the bed and reached for the door.

Then he stopped. He knew what would happen if he invited her into the bedroom. *He knew.* Making love to Rose was all he could think about. Especially here, where there was so much love everywhere. He felt awash in it. Enveloped in love. And he knew it wasn't just the house.

It was Rose. She loved him.

She hadn't spoken the words. But he'd been able to see it on her beautiful face. She'd never learned to lie. Her expressive eyes were an open book for him to read.

She'd seen him at his worst, she knew what he'd done, and yet she loved him. How was it possible?

Clenching his hands into fists, Xerxes took a deep breath. He heard her waiting on the other side of the door, waiting for him to open it and let her in. It was like agony, knowing she was there and still doing nothing. Finally, he heard her give up and her footsteps disappear down the hall.

He exhaled. Closing his eyes, he leaned back against the door.

He wanted her. Now more than ever.

But it was more than that. It had become far more than lust. More then admiration. More even than respect.

She was the most loving woman he'd ever met. Honest. Sweet. Kind. Brave. She was the kind of woman who could make any man—even him—become decent and true, just by the effect of her presence. He loved her.

His body straightened, his eyes opened, wide with shock.

He was in love with her.

Xerxes, a man who had nothing in this world but money and power—nothing of value—had fallen in love with a woman who made everything glorious and new. The most precious, adorable, passionate woman in the world.

He wasn't remotely worthy of her. And yet he ached to be. He ached to take her in his arms, to tell her he loved her, to make her his wife and treasure her forever. Eagerly, he grabbed the door handle.

Then he froze.

He loved her. But he'd made a promise to trade her. A promise that would save a nineteen-year-old girl's life.

He'd made a promise. He had no choice.

But Rose did.

Going back to the window, he swung the lead-paned glass open and took a deep breath of the cold night air.

For once in his life, he would give himself up to someone else's control. To Rose's. The truth was, he admitted quietly to himself, the power had always been hers.

He stared at the moonlight frosting the black ocean waves. From the moment they'd met, he'd thought he'd been the one in control. He'd been her captor; she'd been his prisoner. But she had always been the more powerful one, though neither of them had realized it. And tomorrow, she would decide his fate.

Reaching for his phone, he dialed. The first number

was to his lawyer in San Francisco. The second was a hated number he knew by heart.

"Växborg," he said, "I'm ready to trade."

CHAPTER FOURTEEN

THE next morning, gray rain streaked the windows on the drive north to San Francisco.

Rose wore a black dress and black raincoat, appropriate for either a death in the family or for any woman being traded away like a used car. She glanced for the tenth time at Xerxes sitting beside her in the backseat of the black SUV. He continued to ignore her.

Her family had offered to give them a ride to the airport, but he'd refused, and a half hour later, a black SUV and a full-sized van had roared in front of the old rambling house. Six bodyguards in dark suits had poured out as a uniformed chauffeur opened the door for Xerxes. Her parents' jaws had dropped. So much for *regular folk*!

Today, Rose thought, giving him another nervous side glance. Today, she would tell him she loved him. But not now. No, not yet. Biting her lip, she gripped her hands together, staring down at her lap. The plane ride to Las Vegas would last two hours. There was no need to blurt out her personal feelings in earshot of the chauffeur and bodyguard in the front seat!

Especially since she was already so scared...

She looked out at the passing scenery and gave a

sudden start. Leaning forward, she touched the chauffeur's shoulder timidly. "Excuse me, but you've made a mistake. We're not even close to the city!"

"He hasn't made a mistake," Xerxes said.

She sat back in her seat. "He hasn't?"

"We're not going to the airport."

"We're not?"

He turned to look at her. His eyes were dark. "Do you remember I told you about the medical clinic an hour east of San Francisco? The best brain trauma clinic in the country?"

She stared at him. "We're going to the clinic? Not Las Vegas?"

He nodded.

"You got Laetitia back!" she whispered.

He looked away. "Yes."

Staring at him, a slow feeling of joy rose inside her as she realized what it had to mean.

Xerxes wasn't going to trade her after all. He'd realized he cared about Rose more than his iron-clad promises. He must have gone back on his vow never to pay off Lars, and offered the man a fortune in trade for Laetitia instead of Rose. It was the only solution that made sense!

Xerxes had chosen Rose. He'd decided she was more important to him than his promise!

But as she looked at him, the smile slid from her face. Was that why Xerxes didn't look particularly happy? Because for the first time in his life, he'd broken his word?

The SUV passed a thicket of juniper trees and drove past a gate into the parking lot of a small modern hospital. The building was blocky and sterile, but even in the cold rain of late February, Rose had never seen anything so beautiful.

Xerxes had chosen her. Over his promises. Over honor. It was all she could do not to wrap her arms around herself and sing a happy song. And suddenly, she was so filled with love for him that she no longer cared who heard her.

As the car stopped in front of the hospital, she turned to Xerxes in the backseat.

"I love you," she blurted out.

His black eyes widened. She heard his intake of breath. "Rose—"

She covered his mouth with her hand. "If I don't tell you now, I might never have the courage. I love you, Xerxes. I love you and I'll never forget that today you chose me over…"

Her voice trailed off as she saw a red Ferrari roar past their SUV, followed by a van. The vehicles parked in front of them on the curb. A man got out of the Ferrari, and Rose's eyes widened. Her hand fell numbly into her lap.

"Lars?" Shocked, she turned to Xerxes, her eyes begging for an explanation she could bear. "What is Lars doing here?"

The driver and chauffeur got out of the SUV, closing the doors solidly behind them, and they were alone. Xerxes's face was almost expressionless as he faced her.

"He's here for the trade."

Rose stared at him. "The…trade?"

She turned back to see Lars open the back doors

of the van parked in front of them. Inside, Rose saw a slender, dark-haired woman sleeping on a stretcher. Lars glared at Xerxes, jabbing his thumb toward the unconscious woman, then waited with a sour expression, his hands on his hips.

Then he saw Rose and gave her a sickeningly sweet smile.

Twisting her head away, Rose closed her eyes with a whimper. "You can't trade me. You can't."

"I have no choice."

His cold words went through her soul like a blow.

She'd been a fool to think he'd changed, or that he cared about her. His honor meant more to him than Rose ever could. Her heart fell to her shoes with a dull thud. Blinking fast, she said, "There must be some other way—"

"There is not," he said. "I've tried. Tried and failed. Everywhere I looked for her, I arrived too late. I have no choice but to trade." His dark eyes glittered as he looked up at her. "But what happens next is up to you."

She stared at him in sudden shock.

"Those weren't business trips at all, were they?" she breathed. "The honeymoon cottage in the Maldives. Our villa in Cabo. I thought they were romantic trips we took for your work, but the whole time you were searching for Laetitia behind my back!"

He gave a single jerky nod.

Tears flooded her eyes. "You're no better than Lars," she whispered. "Romancing one woman while committed to another."

"That's not how it was!"

She saw dark pain in Xerxes's eyes, but she was too

hurt to hold back any longer. "Who is Laetitia to you, Xerxes?" she said. "Why do you love her? *Who is she to you?*"

"I can't tell you."

"Because you made a promise."

"Yes."

"And my feelings mean nothing."

"That's not true." He took a deep breath. "But I must fulfill my obligation."

"So that's all I am to you? An obligation?"

"Rose, no," he said. "I…" He looked at her. "I…care for you. Very much."

"You *care* for me," she said bitterly. "Thank you. I've just told you I'm in *love* with you!"

He blinked slowly, then pushed an envelope into her numb hands. "I'm giving you the choice," he said. "I've held you captive, seduced you. Now you have the power. I'm setting you free to decide."

"By trading me?" Tears were brimming over her lashes as she crumpled the envelope in her fist. She could not let herself cry in front of him, could not! "By discarding me, pushing me into another man's arms?"

"No!" he said fiercely. He put his larger hand over hers. "I know you'll never love him again. But…*it must be your choice.*"

The icy reality slowly sank into Rose's heart. Xerxes was really letting her go. He was trading her for the woman he truly loved. And he wouldn't even offer Rose the small comfort of an explanation!

Agony and fury ripped her heart into shreds. She wrenched her hand from his grasp.

"You love promises so much? All right. Here's one

for you." She lifted her chin, her eyes wet with unshed tears. "Never come looking for me, Xerxes. I never want to see you again!"

He sucked in his breath. "You don't mean that."

"Yes, I do. I'll go through with this—this *trade*." Her lip twisted. "But I want your word I'll never see you again."

"No!" He put his hands on her shoulders, searching her eyes with his own. "Don't you understand?" he said in a low voice. "If I make you a promise, I cannot break it."

"I understand that. Better than anyone." She shook his hands off her shoulders and spoke in an icy voice that revealed nothing of her heartbreak. "That's why I want to hear you speak the words."

"I don't want to do it!"

"As you said," she gave him a hard, cold stare, "it's not your choice."

He took a deep breath, closing his eyes.

"Fine." The words were low, as if ripped from his soul. "If that is truly what you wish. I will not come after you. I will not try to see you again."

"Promise!"

"I give you my word." He swallowed. When he opened his eyes, their dark, fathomless pain registered dimly through her numb heart. "But in return," he choked out, "you must promise me you will read that letter."

"Fine." She wrenched away from him, pushing open the car door before he could see her cry.

He'd actually done it. He'd made the promise. Some part of her had hoped, at the last moment, that he would refuse to make it, that he would tell her he loved her and only her.

Her mistake.

Stumbling out of the SUV, she tripped toward the curb, where Lars was waiting for her beside his gleaming sports car. He looked down at her, beaming.

"Darling," the baron cried. "At last, you are back with me."

"I will be a better man from now on. Everything is going to be different now, petal. I swear to you. I will do whatever you say, anything to make you happy, anything at all...."

Rose stared out wearily at the passing scenery as they approached the eastern edge of San Francisco. For the last hour, Lars had been prattling on about forgiveness and love. She didn't think he knew what the hell he was talking about.

But then, neither did she, Rose thought bitterly. She thought of the stark, anguished look on Xerxes's face when he'd said, "I will not try to see you again," and it was all she could do to keep from crying.

So maybe she did finally know what love was after all. *Pain*.

She blinked quickly, staring out at the rain as they zoomed west on the highway.

"I was so selfish to insist on having our wedding in Sweden. I should have realized how important it was to you to be married in your own hometown. I swear to you, petal, this time we'll do it differently...."

"Just take me home," she whispered.

"Absolutely," Lars said, clearly thrilled to get any

response from her. "Straight home to your mother. Then we'll have the wedding you always wanted. As soon as possible. Is tomorrow too soon?"

That statement was so shocking that she turned to gape at him. "You can't honestly think I'm going to marry you?"

He switched lanes in his Ferrari, weaving through traffic on the rainy, slippery highway. "I know this whole experience has been very upsetting for you, petal, forced to endure the captivity of that depraved beast…"

Depraved beast? She had a sudden memory of Xerxes's haunted expression as Lars had driven by him in the Ferrari, with Rose beside him. Her eyes had met Xerxes's in the endless gray rain. Then Lars had stomped on the gas pedal, and they'd left him behind.

Xerxes was lost to her now. Forever.

"But we must put that all unpleasantness behind us now," Lars finished firmly.

With an intake of breath, she whirled back to face him.

"What was *unpleasant*," she said coldly, "was the way you lured me into a fake wedding to try to get me into bed, while you were waiting for your real wife to die so you could steal her money."

Silence fell in the Ferrari.

"I did that because I loved you. I needed money for you. To make you happy," Lars said in a determinedly cheerful voice. "But petal, we must move on now with our lives." He gave her a toothy grin. "Marry me tonight. Let me start making it up to you."

She had a sudden memory of raspberries in champagne, bubble bath, inscrutable dark eyes filled with tenderness and fire.

"What are you doing?"

"Making it up to you," Xerxes had said.

Catching herself, she looked at the blond baron beside her. Lars clearly believed that with almost no effort, he could make her swoon back into his arms. How was it possible she'd ever been so blind as to believe herself in love with such a man?

"We're not getting married," she told him evenly. "Not tonight. Not ever."

"But I did it all out of love for you," he pleaded. "I divorced Laetitia, gave up her fortune. All I have now is this car and a castle that requires a fortune just to maintain. I gave up everything—for you!"

Her eyes narrowed. "And you think that makes me obligated to marry you? Because you allowed Xerxes to get her some decent medical care, when you were waiting eagerly for her to die of your neglect?"

He reached one hand from the steering wheel and tried to take her hand. "You're just angry," he pleaded. "After our wedding…"

"What will it take for you to ever actually listen to me?" she shouted. "I am not going to marry you. Ever! Pull off the highway. I'll take a taxi home!"

He withdrew his hand. His face was grim as he pulled off the highway. But instead of stopping, he turned the car around to drive the opposite direction on the highway, now heading to the east.

"Do you really think I'll let you go?" he said in a low voice. "I gave up Laetitia's fortune. You owe me yours."

"My fortune!" Rose choked out a laugh. "You mean the fifty dollars in my bank account? You can have it!"

"I mean the money Novros gave you," he said coldly. "Millions of dollars and that old factory in the bargain." He switched gears to go faster on the highway. "Once the building is demolished, the land might fetch a good price," he mused. "Perhaps for a gated community of vacation homes."

"What are you talking about?"

"Funny, isn't it? Novros called me last night. He'd always said he'd never give me a penny. But this time, he offered instead to give money to you. *What happens next is up to Rose*, he said." He glanced at her out of the corner of his eye. "Oh, did Novros not tell you? He's just made you a very rich woman."

Rose suddenly thought of the envelope he'd given her, still clenched in her hand. Her hands trembled as she started to open the envelope.

Lars ripped it out of her hands and tossed it out his window.

"Why did you do that?" she gasped.

"You don't need it."

"What?"

"Forget him, Rose."

"Stop this car!"

"Novros is a nameless bastard. A nobody. He's brainwashed you, turned you against me," he said resentfully. "Just as he did that sister of his."

Her mouth fell open. "Laetitia is his *sister*?"

Lars shrugged. "Half sister. Something like that. He kept it quiet. Promised her he wouldn't start a scandal.

Her mother was sickly. After their father's death, Laetitia feared one more shock might kill her." He gave a cold smile. "She was right. Except it was the shock of Laetitia's accident that finally killed the old woman, and left the whole fortune to my bride."

She stared at him in shock. "You're a monster!"

"Now, is that anything to say to the man you love?"

"I don't love you!"

"You will love me, petal," he said, still smiling. He reached out to stroke her cheek. "I promise you that."

When she jerked her head away, Lars looked at her resentfully. "Too good for me now, are you? It disgusts me how you let him touch you."

Turning away, she didn't answer. He stared at her, then stomped harder on the gas pedal. As the car went faster and faster down the highway, she gripped her seat belt in fear.

"You were such a sweet, obedient girl," he said in a low voice. "I'll make you that way again."

He veered abruptly off the highway to a side road, heading toward the distant mountains. The road was rough and bumpy beneath the wide tires of the race car as they flew through the forest. As the rain soon changed to sleet, she stared out the window in a panic as the Ferrari went faster and faster, sliding on the icy, rocky road still covered with scattered snow.

Xerxes, she thought, closing her eyes. *Please come for me.*

Then she remembered the promise she'd forced on him and nearly wept. Perhaps he'd have immediately forgotten Rose from the instant he had his sick half sister back in his arms, desperately needing his care. But the promise Rose had forced him to give her had been the nail in the coffin. Xerxes now couldn't come save her, even if he'd wanted to. She'd made sure of that. And now it would destroy her.

You were right, she whispered silently. The one time Rose had been hurt enough to try for revenge, it had caused her more pain than she'd ever imagined possible.

Turning to face Lars, she choked out, "Where are you taking me?"

"A private cabin where we can be alone. For days. Weeks, if necessary." Lars gave her a sensual smile that made her shudder as he purred, "I'll make you remember your love for me. I'll enjoy your silky body. And when I've cleansed you of that Greek bastard's memory, you will give me everything and marry me."

CHAPTER FIFTEEN

"WE'RE still running tests, Mr. Novros, but we're optimistic."

Xerxes sagged in relief against the white concrete wall of the medical clinic. "Thank God."

"We'll keep you updated." The doctor looked at him with concern. "But you should get some rest. Before we have to check you in here as well."

"I'm fine."

The doctor clapped him on the shoulder encouragingly. "Don't worry. She's young and strong. Her chances are excellent for a full recovery."

After he'd left, Xerxes closed his eyes, feeling the fresh drizzle of rain on his face. His sister was safe. Laetitia was now receiving the best medical care possible. For the first time in a year, he did not have that driving fear inside him, the fear that he might fail her, the fear that she might die after he'd promised to always look out for her.

He should have been overcome with relief and joy. And yet he found himself still hunched over with grief. He looked up to see a blond woman coming out of the mist in the parking lot.

"Rose," he whispered, his heart in his throat. Had she read the letter? Had she changed her mind?

Then he saw the blonde embrace another man, a male nurse who'd just come out of the clinic. Looking at her more closely, Xerxes realized the woman looked nothing like Rose. His vision was playing tricks on him.

She'd told him she loved him. And for his answer, he'd traded her. He'd given her into Växborg's hands.

Had she read the letter yet? Would she keep her promise?

His hands clenched into fists as he rubbed his stinging eyes. All he wanted was to have Rose in his arms, to share his joy about his half sister's prognosis. For Christ's sake, to even tell her that Laetitia was his sister!

Instead, he'd made a promise he never wanted to keep. He was powerless to pursue her. And now he was a prisoner of his own word.

Maybe it was for the best, he told himself wearily. God knew Rose deserved better than a man like him. She deserved a husband with an open, loving heart, an equal partner who would share everything with her— not a closed-off, vengeful man with a scarred heart like Xerxes.

But I can change, his heart cried. *I already have changed, because of her.*

All he wanted was for her to be happy. And the last time he'd seen her, her face had been so wan and pale, her eyes so sad, as she'd driven past him in the Ferrari with Växborg at her side. The baron, on the other hand, had looked smug and satisfied.

And something more.

Xerxes blinked. What had been in the man's eyes? He'd been too distracted by worry and grief to pay much attention to Växborg at the time, but now there'd been something in the man's expression. He'd dismissed Växborg as a weakling. But even a weakling could be vicious when cornered.

Trying to tell himself he had nothing to worry about, Xerxes reached for his cell phone. His hands shook as he dialed the number of her parents' house an hour to the south.

But when Vera answered on the third ring, she sounded bewildered at his questions. "Rose? No, we haven't seen her. No, she hasn't called. Why? What's wrong? We thought she was with you!"

"I'll explain later," Xerxes replied, but when he hung up his whole body was cold with sweat.

Rose would not have willingly run off with Växborg. She detested the man's lack of morals, his selfish cruelty. She would have wanted to go straight home to her family. She wouldn't have detoured for a cozy chat with the baron.

At least not willingly.

Xerxes raked his black hair back with his hand. How could he have been so arrogant as to assume that Växborg was no threat, and he would meekly accept Rose's refusal? How could he have believed the man would relinquish her—and her new fortune—without a fight?

The man's weakness, his cowardice, were exactly what made him dangerous. And now Xerxes could do nothing to save her.

Sucking in his breath, he punched the concrete wall

of the clinic, causing little pieces of rock to crumble and scatter. Blood oozed from his knuckles as he covered his face with his hands. He was helpless to find the woman he loved.

Or was he?

Slowly, he lowered his hands.

All his life, he'd considered his promise to be his worth as a man. But in this moment, he realized that there was something even more sacred than a man's word.

His love.

It was honor beyond any promise: *A man had to protect his woman.*

He had to keep Rose safe.

Opening his cell phone, he dialed his chief body-guard, his top private investigators, his connections in San Francisco, even the sheriff in Rose's hometown. No car accidents had been reported. As he waited for news, Xerxes paced back and forth in the parking lot of the medical clinic. He no longer felt the cold drizzle of the rain against his face. His muscles ached to jump into his car and drive to find her. *But where? Which direction should he go?*

Lars wouldn't take her to a motel. He wouldn't take her anywhere she might be seen. And he no longer had the money to charter a plane.

Unless he married Rose. Xerxes had thought it was such a tidy way to get revenge on Lars, to use the man's arrogance and greed against him, to get Laetitia to safety while allowing Rose to make her own choice about her life. He raked his hair back again. He'd been a fool!

The phone rang in his hands and he answered on the first ring. "Yes?"

"A red Ferrari was seen on the I-50, heading east," the investigator told him. "No license plate information, but a car like that stands out."

Heading east. Why east? There was nothing in that direction, nothing but the wild mountains and eventually Lake Tahoe, which in February would still be thick with snow and frozen rain. Why would anyone be insane enough to drive a low-slung race car in that direction? Where was the man going?

Then Xerxes knew.

Closing his phone with an intake of breath, he ran for his SUV.

"Get in there!"

Cursing, Lars shoved her into the old cabin before he slammed the door behind them. Rose backed away, still glaring at him, rubbing her half-frozen wrists that he'd bruised with his sinewy grip.

They'd walked for three hours in the frozen rain, up the snowy, rutted dirt road on foot after Lars's Ferrari had slid on a patch of ice and blown a tire. Her black dress and thin black coat couldn't hold up against these wintry conditions. Her black leather pumps were soaked through, her feet like ice, and she'd almost forgotten what it was like to be warm. She didn't know if she would ever feel warm again.

But still, when Rose had seen the cabin in the clearing, she'd tried to run away. She'd turned blindly back toward the woods to take her chances in the frozen mountains. But Lars had had other ideas. Now, he blocked the door, locking it behind him.

"What is this place?" she choked out, huddling near the cold fireplace.

"Laetitia's great-grandfather built it." He looked around with a twist of scorn on his lip. "I left my wife here with an incompetent nurse right after her accident. I hoped I would return from San Francisco and find she'd joined her mother in the afterlife. No such luck. My wife—" he spat out the word "—still lived."

Lars picked up a piece of the wood stacked neatly by the fireplace. "This is who their family really is," he said. "Jumped-up nobodies. Peasants who earned money with their hands. Like *Novros*."

Rose sucked in her breath. Xerxes's name hit her like a blow. *If only...*

"He came here last year, hot on my heels," he said coldly. "He very nearly found Laetitia. I barely had time to pull her into the woods with the nurse to hide. After he left, I started leaving false trails around the world, hiring look-alikes to distract him."

She thought of all the anguished energy that Xerxes had spent trying to find his sister. "How could you be so cruel?" she demanded.

He shrugged. "It was easier to keep him on a hopeless wild-goose chase than risk moving Laetitia away from here." He added in a sullen voice, "I thought the car accident was fate finally rewarding me as I deserved. I never thought she would live for a whole year."

Rose stared at him, her eyes wide, her hand covering her mouth as she whispered, "You're truly a monster. You tried to kill your own wife!"

"No," he bit out. "No one can say I tried to kill her. All I did was help fate. She should have died. I deserve her money more than she ever did. She married me. I earned it. I deserve it." He looked at her. "Just as I deserve you."

With an intake of breath at the hard hunger in his eyes, Rose took a step back.

Lars must have seen the fear in her expression, because he turned back to the fireplace in a posture of confidence. Leaning forward to open the flue, he placed a single log inside and lit a match. He pressed the flame up against the wood.

Without any tinder, the log wouldn't light. All Lars succeeded in doing was burning his fingers as the flame burned down. As Rose watched, he lit four matches all to the same result, and with every failure his anger grew.

Finally, with a curse, he blew out the fifth match and tossed it to the floor. He glared at Rose, who was hiding her incredulous expression with her hands.

His scowl changed to a sensual, threatening smile.

"I'll start the fire later," he purred. "In the meantime—I'll just warm myself with you."

He lunged toward her. With a yelp, she tried to run away, but he was too fast for her. Grabbing her, he pushed her against the kitchen table.

She fought him with a scream. When she bit the hand he placed over her mouth, he roughly turned her over on her belly.

"This will only hurt at first," he said, panting. "Then you will realize you love it."

"No!" she screamed, thrashing.

"Stop fighting!" he yelled. Brutally, he grabbed her by her hair then banged her head against the hard wooden table. She went limp, dazed as she saw stars.

"Once you're pregnant with my child," he panted, "you will accept me as your husband." Unzipping his fly, he started to lift up her dress. "You will—"

His voice ended with a choke as he dropped her.

Weakly, Rose turned around against the table and she saw a miracle: Xerxes had him by the throat.

"You like to hurt women you claim to love," Xerxes said in cold, deadly fury. "You deserve to die."

"No, please," Lars cried. "No—"

Mercilessly, Xerxes punched him in the face, knocking him to the rough wooden floor. Lars dropped like a stone.

"Xerxes," Rose whimpered.

With an intake of breath, Xerxes went to her, gathering her up tenderly in his arms.

"Rose, oh, Rose," he breathed, holding her. "Oh, my darling. Did he hurt you? My God, tell me I was in time!"

"He didn't hurt me. You came," she whispered, touching his face in wonder. "Oh, Xerxes, somehow you came."

"Rose, I have to tell you something. I…"

Lars got up behind them, then with a last shouted curse he stumbled for the door. Flinging it open, he ran out of the cabin, heading for the snowy forest.

Xerxes started to chase him, but Rose grabbed his hand.

"No, please," she whispered. Her cold fingers curled around his. "Please stay with me."

"Yes." He instantly turned back to her. "You're so cold," he murmured in a worried voice. He pulled her back against his chest, wrapping his coat around her. "I have to get you warm."

Rose looked up at him. Cold? She wasn't cold any longer. Dawning joy was slowly thawing her heart from within. "You broke your promise," she said in shock. "You came for me."

"I came." He drew back, looking down at her with troubled dark eyes. "Forgive me."

"Forgive you?" She laughed even as tears streaked down her face. "For saving my life? All right. Just this time, I will."

But his eyes were serious. "I always prided myself on keeping my word above all else. But today I realized honor means nothing without love. Without *you*."

Xerxes gently stroked her face, tilting her chin upward.

"I love you, Rose," he said in a low voice, searching her eyes intently. "Tell me it's not too late. Tell me I have a chance to win you back. I love you. I love you so much."

Her heart ached at the words she'd waited a lifetime to hear, from the man she'd waited a lifetime to find. The strong, honorable, noble man she could love for the rest of her life.

Reaching her hand up against his rough cheek, she felt warmth and joy overwhelming her heart. "I never stopped loving you," she whispered. "I will love you forever."

Looking down at her, his black eyes were suspiciously wet. "Marry me, Rose."

In answer, she nodded as tears streaked her face.

He sucked in his breath. As he lowered his mouth to hers, he whispered, "You are my family. My wife. My love. You...*you* are my promise."

Two months later, Rose stepped out of the white clapboard chapel into the spring sunshine, still gripping her new husband's hand.

"It stopped raining," Xerxes said in amazement, looking up at the fluffy clouds in the blue sky. "Is that the sun?"

Was he implying that his new home in northern California wasn't exactly the sunniest place in the world? She grinned at him, her heart full of love. "I wouldn't know. Every day seems sunny to me," she said over the lump in her throat, "as long as I'm with you."

His dark eyes caressed her. Lifting her left hand to his lips, he gently kissed her fingers, and her simple gold wedding ring.

Family and friends followed them outside, cheering and throwing flower petals as Rose and Xerxes headed for the car waiting to take them to the airport. They had no time to attend their own wedding reception; they barely had time for their honeymoon. Resting her hand on his arm, Rose looked at her incredibly handsome husband with a sigh of regret. "I'm sorry we only have two days to spend in Mexico."

He grinned at her. "We'll make it count."

"And missing our reception—"

"Rose." He put his hand over hers. "A wedding is just a single day. We have the rest of our lives to celebrate our love together."

She looked up at him gratefully. "I promise once Linden Candy is off the ground," she vowed, "I'll take you somewhere romantic for a full month."

"My wife, the business tycoon," he teased. "I can see I'm going to have to step it up just to keep up with you."

In the last two months, she'd rebuilt and refurbished the old factory, installing brand-new equipment. She'd hired back most of the old crew, except for one former CEO who'd flatly refused.

"I'll only be available for meetings on the golf course, sweetie," her father had said with a laugh, then he'd put his hand on her shoulder. "I'm proud of you, Rose. This is what you've worked for."

She intended to get national distribution of their signature nostalgic taffies, but she also wanted to create new candy bars for a more modern palate. She grinned. She could hardly wait to get started on candy research and development. But then, she'd been craving sweets even more than usual lately.

In front of the vintage 1930s Ford decked in flowers, Xerxes pulled her into his arms. By the look in his eyes, they would barely have time to reach the airport before the honeymoon started.

With the whole town watching, he lowered his mouth to hers, searing her body with his rough embrace, until she was surprised the ladylike vintage wedding dress she'd borrowed from her mother didn't burst into flame.

"Get a room!" her youngest brother yelled.

"Let them enjoy themselves," one of her sisters hissed. "A honeymoon only happens once in a lifetime!"

A new voice chimed in, "Yeah, get a room!"

Blushing bashfully, Rose pulled away. She smiled at Laetitia, Xerxes's nineteen-year-old sister, who was watching them and laughing from her wheelchair. Laetitia was in physical therapy, growing stronger every day. Just last week she'd managed to take her first steps. The doctors expected a full recovery.

Lars Växborg, however, hadn't been so lucky. He'd apparently lost his way in the snowy wilderness near Lake Tahoe, and hadn't been found again—until spring thaw. Rose felt bad for him. Almost.

"Throw the bouquet!" one of her old friends from high school called. "Throw it this way, Rosie!"

Turning away, Rose tossed the bouquet recklessly behind her. Whirling back around, she was shocked to see who'd caught it, but not nearly as shocked as her youngest brother Tom, a football player, who must have grabbed it by pure instinct. He stared down at the bouquet of pink roses in horror.

Rose laughed until she cried. As her new husband led her toward the limousine, she said wistfully, "I wish we could stay for the reception."

"I wish we were already at our honeymoon," Xerxes growled in reply. "I want to see you in that bikini."

"I don't know about a bikini," she said, glancing at him out of the corner of her eye. "I've gained ten pounds since our last time in Mexico."

"In all the right places." As she smacked his shoulder in mock rage, he pulled back to thoroughly look at her. "I can't get enough of you," he murmured, and he kissed her again. When he pulled away, he gasped, "Forget the beach. We'll just get margaritas delivered to our room."

She took a deep breath. "I can't."

"Champagne, then."

"I can't do that, either." With a mischievous smile, she stood on her tiptoes and whispered in his ear, "I'm pregnant."

Jerking back, he stared down at her in shock. "You're—what?"

"You're going to be a father," she said happily.

He gaped at her, unable to speak.

Rose's smile faltered. "I know we talked about waiting to start a family until my company was up and running, but it just happened." She bit her lip. "Is it all right? I mean—do you mind?"

He stared at her, then he exploded.

"Do I mind?" he yelled.

His handsome face was bright with thrilled wonder and delight. Lifting her in his arms with a whoop of joy, he swung her in her wedding dress, spinning her around and around in front of the chapel, until her white satin slippers soared into the blue sky. His joy caused the birds to fly into the air, bursting toward the sun.

And as she tumbled back into her husband's passionate embrace, Rose knew just how they felt.

Real love in real life—that was the fairy tale. That was the promise that could never be broken.

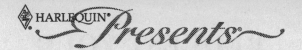

REQUEST YOUR
FREE BOOKS!

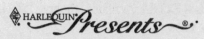 HARLEQUIN *Presents* ®

2 FREE NOVELS PLUS
2 FREE GIFTS!

YES! Please send me 2 FREE Harlequin Presents® novels and my 2 FREE gifts (gifts are worth about $10). After receiving them, if I don't wish to receive any more books, I can return the shipping statement marked "cancel." If I don't cancel, I will receive 6 brand-new novels every month and be billed just $4.05 per book in the U.S. or $4.74 per book in Canada. That's a saving of at least 15% off the cover price! It's quite a bargain! Shipping and handling is just 50¢ per book.* I understand that accepting the 2 free books and gifts places me under no obligation to buy anything. I can always return a shipment and cancel at any time. Even if I never buy another book, the two free books and gifts are mine to keep forever.

106/306 HDN E5M4

Name	(PLEASE PRINT)
Address	Apt. #
City	State/Prov.	Zip/Postal Code

Signature (if under 18, a parent or guardian must sign)

Mail to the **Harlequin Reader Service:**
IN U.S.A.: P.O. Box 1867, Buffalo, NY 14240-1867
IN CANADA: P.O. Box 609, Fort Erie, Ontario L2A 5X3

Not valid for current subscribers to Harlequin Presents books.

Are you a current subscriber to Harlequin Presents books and want to receive the larger-print edition? Call 1-800-873-8635 today!

* Terms and prices subject to change without notice. Prices do not include applicable taxes. N.Y. residents add applicable sales tax. Canadian residents will be charged applicable provincial taxes and GST. Offer not valid in Quebec. This offer is limited to one order per household. All orders subject to approval. Credit or debit balances in a customer's account(s) may be offset by any other outstanding balance owed by or to the customer. Please allow 4 to 6 weeks for delivery. Offer available while quantities last.

Your Privacy: Harlequin Books is committed to protecting your privacy. Our Privacy Policy is available online at www.eHarlequin.com or upon request from the Reader Service. From time to time we make our lists of customers available to reputable third parties who may have a product or service of interest to you. If you would prefer we not share your name and address, please check here. ☐

Help us get it right—We strive for accurate, respectful and relevant communications. To clarify or modify your communication preferences, visit us at www.ReaderService.com/consumerschoice.

HP10R

HARLEQUIN®

A Romance

FOR EVERY MOOD™

Spotlight on

Classic

Quintessential, modern love stories
that are romance at its finest.

See the next page
to enjoy a sneak peek from
the Harlequin® Romance series.

*Harlequin Romance author Donna Alward is loved
for her gorgeous rancher heroes.*

*Meet Wyatt as he's confronted by both a precious
little pink bundle left on his doorstep and his neighbor Elli
who's going to show him the ropes....*

Introducing
PROUD RANCHER, PRECIOUS BUNDLE

THE SQUAWKING QUIETED as Elli picked the baby up, and
Wyatt turned around, trying hard to ignore the feelings of
inadequacy as Darcy immediately stopped fussing.

"Maybe she's uncomfortable. What do you think, sweet-
heart?" Elli turned her conversation to the baby.

"What do you think is wrong?" Wyatt asked, putting the
coffee pot back on the burner.

A strange look passed over Elli's face, one that looked
like guilt and panic. But it was gone quickly. "I couldn't
say," she replied.

"But you were so good with her this afternoon." Wyatt
put his hands on his hips.

"Lucky, that's all. I just…remembered a few things."
The same strange look flitted over her features once more.

Wyatt took the coffee to the table. "You fooled me. You
looked like you knew exactly what you were doing." So
much so that Wyatt had felt completely inept. A feeling he
despised. He was used to being the one in control.

Elli and Darcy walked the length of the kitchen and
back. After a few moments, she admitted, "I haven't really
cared for a baby before. The things I thought of were simply
things I'd heard about. Not from experience, Mr. Black."

Her chin jutted up, closing the subject but making him

want to ask the questions now pulsing through his mind. But then he remembered the old saying—*Don't look a gift horse in the mouth*. He'd benefit from whatever insight she had and be glad of it.

"I don't really know what babies need," he said. "I fed her, patted her back like you did, walked her to sleep, but every time I put her down…"

Wyatt almost groaned. Of course. He'd forgotten one important thing. He'd been so focused on getting the formula the right temperature that he'd forgotten to check her diaper. Not that he had any clue what to do there either.

Pulling calves and shoveling out stalls was far less intimidating than one tiny newborn.

"She's probably due for a diaper change, isn't she." He tried to sound nonchalant. This was a perfect opportunity. Elli must know how to change a diaper. He could simply watch her so he'd know better for the next time.

Instead, Elli came around the corner of the counter and placed Darcy back in his arms. "Here you go, Uncle Wyatt," she said lightly. "You get diaper duty. I'll fix the coffee. Cream and sugar?"

Oh boy, Wyatt thought, looking down into Darcy's pursed face, his smug plan blown to smithereens. He was in for it now.

Will sparks fly between Elli and Wyatt?

Find out in
PROUD RANCHER, PRECIOUS BUNDLE
Available February 2011 from Harlequin Romance

Try these Healthy and Delicious Spring Rolls!

INGREDIENTS

2 packages rice-paper
spring roll wrappers
(20 wrappers)

1 cup grated carrot

¼ cup bean sprouts

1 cucumber, julienned

1 red bell pepper, without
stem and seeds, julienned

4 green onions
finely chopped—
use only the green part

DIRECTIONS

1. Soak one rice-paper wrapper
   in a large bowl of hot water
   until softened.

2. Place a pinch each of carrots,
   sprouts, cucumber, bell
   pepper and green onion on the
   wrapper toward the bottom
   third of the rice paper.

3. Fold ends in and roll tightly
   to enclose filling.

4. Repeat with remaining
   wrappers. Chill before
   serving.

Find this and many more delectable recipes
including the perfect dipping sauce in

YOUR BEST BODY NOW
by
TOSCA RENO
WITH STACY BAKER

Bestselling Author of
THE EAT-CLEAN DIET

Available wherever books are sold!